Lowcountry Getaway

Praise for the Liz Talbot Mystery Series

"Plenty of secrets, long-simmering feuds, and greedy ventures make for a captivating read... Boyer's chick lit PI debut charmingly showcases South Carolina island culture."

— LIBRARY JOURNAL

"Boyer delivers a beach read filled with quirky, endearing characters and a masterfully layered mystery, all set in the lush lowcountry. Don't miss this one!"

— MARY ALICE MONROE, NEW YORK TIMES BESTSELLING AUTHOR

"Has everything you could want in a traditional mystery: a credible and savvy protagonist, a meaty mystery, and setting that will make you want to spend time in South Carolina. I enjoyed every minute of it."

— CHARLAINE HARRIS, NEW YORK TIMES BESTSELLING AUTHOR

"Imaginative, empathetic, genuine, and fun, *Lowcountry Boil* is a lowcountry delight."

— CAROLYN HART, AUTHOR OF THE
BAILEY RUTH RAEBURN SERIES

"The local foods sound scrumptious and the locale descriptions are enough to entice us to be tourists...the PI detail is as convincing as Grafton."

— FRESH FICTION

"Boyer deftly shapes characters with just enough idiosyncrasies without succumbing to cliches while infusing her lighthearted plot with an insightful look at families."

— OLINE COGDILL, SOUTH FLORIDA
SUN SENTINEL

"This light-hearted and authentically Southern mystery is full of heart, insight, and a deep understanding of human nature. Susan M. Boyer is a fresh new voice in crime fiction!"

— HANK PHILLIPPI RYAN, AUTHOR OF
HER PERFECT LIFE

"It's a simmering gumbo of a story full of spice, salt, heat, and shrimp. She had me guessing, detouring for a few laughs then doubling back for another clue right until the last chapter."

— THE HUFFINGTON POST

"Twisted humor has long been a tradition in Southern literature (maybe it's the heat and humidity), and Boyer delivers it with both barrels. In lesser hands, all the hijinks could be distracting, but not in *Lowcountry Boil*. Boyer's voice is so perky that no matter what looney mayhem her characters commit, we happily dive in with them. An original and delightful read."

— BETTY WEBB, *MYSTERY SCENE MAGAZINE*

"Susan Boyer delivers big time with a witty mystery that is fun, radiant, and impossible to put down. I love this book!"

— DARYNDA JONES, NEW YORK TIMES BESTSELLING AUTHOR

"*Lowcountry Bombshell* is that rare combination of suspense, humor, seduction, and mayhem, an absolute must-read not only for mystery enthusiasts but for anyone who loves a fast-paced, well-written story!"

— CASSANDRA KING, AUTHOR OF
THE SAME SWEET GIRLS

The Liz Talbot Mystery Series

Lowcountry Boil (A Liz Talbot Mystery # 1)

Lowcountry Bombshell (A Liz Talbot Mystery # 2)

Lowcountry Boneyard (A Liz Talbot Mystery # 3)

Postcards From Stella Maris (Five Liz Talbot Short Stories)

Lowcountry Bordello (A Liz Talbot Mystery # 4)

Lowcountry Book Club (A Liz Talbot Mystery # 5)

Lowcountry Bonfire (A Liz Talbot Mystery # 6)

Lowcountry Bookshop (A Liz Talbot Mystery # 7)

Lowcountry Boomerang (A Liz Talbot Mystery # 8)

Lowcountry Boondoggle (A Liz Talbot Mystery # 9)

Lowcountry Boughs of Holly (A Liz Talbot Mystery # 10)

Lowcountry Getaway (A Liz Talbot Mystery # 11)

Lowcountry Getaway

A LIZ TALBOT MYSTERY
BOOK ELEVEN

SUSAN M. BOYER

STELLA MARIS BOOKS
LLC

Lowcountry Getaway

A Liz Talbot Mystery

First Edition | December 2022

Stella Maris Books, LLC

https://stellamarisbooksllc.com

Cover design by Elizabeth Mackey

Author photograph by Mic Smith

ISBN-13: 978-1-959023-08-1

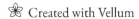 Created with Vellum

For my readers...
Wishing you all the joy, peace, and love of the season
Merry Christmas 2022, y'all!

Chapter One

The dead are vigilant.

I had no idea, until right after Gram passed away a few years back, but my best friend Colleen has been keeping watch over me ever since she died the spring of our junior year in high school. Well, she says she went through a training period first. It's not just me she minds. Her after-life mission is to protect Stella Maris, the island near Charleston, South Carolina, where we grew up. By keeping the pristine island we call home from being overdeveloped, she protects everyone who lives there. We're connected to the Isle of Palms by ferry, you see. Evacuating the island when a hurricane is bearing down on us can be a challenge. The more people who live on the island, the more difficult it is to get everyone out of harm's way.

Colleen protects our twenty-four square mile

Mayberry in paradise by handpicking members for our town council who like things just the way they are. She assists them in getting elected or appointed—mostly without their knowledge—and then protects them from all manner of calamity. I should add here that it's not that we don't welcome visitors in Stella Maris. We'd just like them to rent houses or stay at the Stella Maris Hotel, or Sullivan's Bed and Breakfast, and not build condos, time-shares, and all such as that.

Because my immediate family included two members of the town council—me and my daddy—and my brother Blake was the chief of police, Colleen spent a fair amount of her time with us. It helped that all three of us were not only fans of preserving Stella Maris's small-town charm, but epically stubborn. We'll get back to Colleen in a minute.

So, my husband, Nate, meticulously planned a family getaway for the better part of a year. He brought our entire family to St. John, in the U.S. Virgin Islands, to celebrate our one-year anniversary, Christmas, and a slew of other happy milestones. We had much to be grateful for. Apparently, Nate was quite wealthy, something the terms of his grandfather's will required him to keep from me until our first anniversary. I was still processing exactly how much we had to be grateful for.

If you've never been to St. John, it's the smallest of the three U.S. Virgin Islands. At roughly twenty-eight square miles, it's slightly larger than Stella Maris, but the topography is very different. It's lush and hilly, reminds me of a rainforest, like someone set a piece of the North Carolina mountains (another favorite place of mine) on top of this unspoiled island in the middle of the bluest, clearest water you've ever seen. Two-thirds of the island is a national park, which helps keep this island from being overdeveloped. Some would argue parts of the island are sprouting too many condos, and I wouldn't argue against them. But most of this island paradise still runs wild and green, covered in dense vegetation. I like to think someone like Colleen watches over St. John.

There's no airport in St. John. We flew into St. Thomas, rented Jeeps, and drove them across St. Thomas to Red Hook on the east end, then took the car ferry over to St. John. This was somewhat of an adventure in and of itself, especially with our bunch. We're all accustomed to car ferries, of course. But the one we took from Red Hook over to St. John was a bit more rustic than the Stella Maris ferry, and the waves much more active. Merry slipped Mamma one of her little yellow pills when we left the airport, as a preventative measure.

I'd been looking forward to our trip for months. If you'd told me before we left for St. John that Mamma would make fast friends with two ladies from the Upstate, and that these three sweet Southern belles would embroil us all in a case involving adultery, junk cars, and money laundering, I would've politely inquired as to which hallucinogenic you were imbibing. But that's exactly what happened.

It all started on a Wednesday, two days before Christmas, at Trunk Bay. *Conde Nast Traveler* magazine ranks the beach as one of the top ten on the planet, and I have to say I've never seen a prettier one. It's situated along the north shore of St. John. The sapphire water and white sand are the stuff of postcards and daydreams. There are many lovely beaches on St. John, and we planned to visit them all at least once while we were here, but Trunk Bay is surely a slice of Heaven itself.

We were staying in a truly stunning home named Cinnamon Ridge up on the hillside overlooking Cinnamon Bay, the British Virgin Islands, and a few smaller islets I needed to learn the names of, since I'd recently found out that my husband owned this house with the spectacular views. He and I stayed there on our honeymoon, but he didn't mention it was *his* house at the time. There were a great many things my husband failed to mention, but I digress.

If you look to the left from Cinnamon Ridge you can see Trunk Bay. But the house sits high on a hill, and, like most houses on St. John, doesn't have direct beach access. For that, we'd piled in the Jeeps early that morning and carefully motored down the mountainous road that St. Johnians called Highway 206 and Mamma compared to a goat path—she wasn't far off—and along the North Shore Road to the Trunk Bay parking lot.

Bartholomew Smalls, a large, muscular, Black man, with a bald head, who I'd recently mistaken for a criminal stalker, (in my defense, he was a stranger to me at the time, and he *was* following me) but who actually worked for Nate in security, and was along for the holiday ride, set up chairs on the beach lickety-split while we meandered along the path, past the bath houses, the snack bar, and down the beach. In no time, a semicircle of bright blue zero gravity recliners appeared around a couple of large coolers.

We settled in to soak up the beauty. We didn't have the beach to ourselves that morning, but there was plenty of space between us and the couple to the left and the family to the right. A line of sea grapes, palm trees, and I don't know what all bordered the beach and offered dappled morning shade. Gentle waves of crystal-clear water lapped the shore. A sailboat drifted by. Lush green islets dotted the band of the Atlantic Ocean directly in front of us. It was positively idyllic.

As I mentioned, Colleen takes her duties quite seriously. She'd come with us on vacation, bless her heart. At that particular moment, Colleen stood guard over my family from a hammock between two palm trees. She was also curating our music selection, skipping songs in my playlist she didn't particularly care for, and repeating the ones she did. Just then, "Old Blue Chair" by Kenny Chesney played softly through the Bluetooth speaker I'd set by one of the coolers, blending with the lazy surf.

From the chair beside me, Nate reached out and took

my hand. I smiled at my husband, luxuriating in the moment. All was right with the world.

We spent the morning alternating between snorkeling along the underwater snorkel trail, frolicking on the gentle waves with a variety of colorful noodles, and basking in the tropical sun. At lunchtime, we pulled a picnic from the cooler, and feasted on an array of sandwiches, chips, fruit, and brownies. Afterwards, we meandered down the beach as far as we could go. When we reached the rocky point that separated Trunk Bay from Jumbie Bay, we turned around and walked the length of the beach in the other direction.

"This is just heavenly," said Merry.

"It's positively paradise," said Poppy. "I just love how it feels so wild and unspoiled, yet you still have convenient restrooms."

"Not all the beaches here will have those," said Nate. I could tell my husband was pondering how we'd manage with several high maintenance women at Waterlemon Cay, our favorite snorkeling spot, which featured a half-mile hike in and no facilities.

"Y'all can just leave me by the pool anytime you feel the need to head out into the wilderness," said Mamma. "Or drop me right here."

"I could spend every day here," said Poppy.

"It is gorgeous," I said. "But there are plenty of other gorgeous places to see. It's hard to choose a favorite."

"I don't guess anyone has checked on the hound dog this morning, have they?" asked Daddy.

"Moon Unit is taking excellent care of Chumley and Rhett," I said. "We don't need to call and check on them every day. It's not like they can come to the phone."

"Why can't they?" Daddy gave me a look that challenged my attempt at common sense.

"Oh, Frank," said Mamma. "Moon Unit will call if there's a problem. Relax and enjoy your vacation."

"Should've brought them with us," mumbled Daddy.

"*Frank.*" Mamma shot him a warning look.

I knew what she was thinking and so did he. He hushed up.

"I so enjoyed last night's dinner," said Mamma. "Perhaps we could have Aunt Odella's Famous Brisket again while we're here."

I was somewhat surprised by this. Nate and I loved Aunt Odella's Famous Brisket, a food stand in Cruz Bay near the ferry dock. But it was little more than a lean-to, and I'd half expected Mamma to object to eating there the first time. She's persnickety when it comes to a clean kitchen, and while I'm sure Aunt Odella's is spotless, it's a bit rustic, which might've given Mamma a wrong idea.

"That was as good a brisket as I've ever had," said Blake. "I could eat some more of that."

"You won't get an argument from me," said Nate. "We should eat at Uncle Joe's Barbecue too. It's right beside Aunt Odella's, and every bit as good, but Uncle Joe cooks pork barbecue, ribs, and chicken."

"And wasn't she just the sweetest thing?" asked Merry.

"Aunt Odella?" asked Mamma. "She's positively precious. I love meeting restauranteurs and hearing their stories. She's had an amazing life. Her family's lived here in St. John as far back as they have records. I'd love to have that brisket recipe. She said it has been in her family for five generations. Perhaps if I have another taste, I can figure out what all she marinates it in. And those biscuits... I've never had a flakier biscuit in my entire life."

"Now that's saying something," said Daddy.

Mamma squinted at him. "Exactly what do you mean by that?"

"You're an expert on biscuits, of course." Daddy's tone was frosted with innocence.

Mamma continued to stare at him, searching for the taunt she was certain he intended.

"Aunt Odella's been here as long as I've been coming to St. John," said Nate. "Probably a lot longer. She's an institution. She also operates a floating bar on the other side of the island. She's quite the successful entrepreneur."

When we'd made it back to our chairs, Bartholomew handed us all refreshing beverages from the massive blue cooler, and we settled in to enjoy the view some more. The afternoon sun made me lazy, and I may have drifted into a daze. I was peripherally aware, when Mamma called out to Bartholomew, that it wasn't the first time she'd done it.

"Bartholomew?" Mamma said to the man she assumed was along to attend to such things as umbrellas and chairs. Why wouldn't she think that? Mamma had no idea—none of them did—that Nate was worth enough money that kidnapping was a legitimate concern. I'd only just learned that myself, was still trying to come to grips with it all. It was more than a little surreal. We were still deciding if we wanted to share this news with our family. Money oftentimes complicates things, has adverse effects on relationships.

One thing I had made note of: my husband's financial situation was not news to Colleen. She wasn't surprised in the least to hear about the money. But she hadn't seen fit to clue me in. I'm digressing again.

Bartholomew walked towards Mamma's beach chair. "Yes, ma'am. What can I do for you, Miss Carolyn?" He was a good-natured soul. He'd been pampering Mamma since we left the Lowcountry on a private jet. I was reasonably certain all of this was a dream from which I would awaken at any moment.

Mamma smiled up at Bartholomew. "I'm terribly sorry to bother you again. You are so sweet to look after us. Would you be so kind as to adjust my sunshade? I'm afraid I'm getting sun on my face again."

"Yes ma'am. We can't have you gettin' burned." He moved the built-in shade an inch to the left. "How's that?"

"Oh that's perfect," said Mamma. "Thank you so much."

"Anyone else need an adjustment?" Bartholomew scanned our arc of high-tech beach chairs.

Everyone else murmured their no thank yous, and Bartholomew returned to his seat.

"How much do we pay Bartholomew?" I asked Nate the fourth time Mamma asked Bartholomew to adjust her sunshade.

"Double for the trip," said Nate.

"I'm worried that's not enough."

"He's got backup coming, someone else from the team. These aren't Bart's typical duties, sure enough. But unless and until we decide to bring everyone fully up to speed, we can't really explain his presence any other way. So far, he seems to be handling it with good humor."

"Someone else from the team? Exactly how many people are on the team?" I'd only met Bartholomew very early Sunday morning—three days ago—just after Nate told me about the money. Apparently, recent events had induced him to hire private security.

"Hmm," said Nate, like maybe he didn't want to get into all that just then. "I think you need some more sunscreen. The sun's rays are closer to the earth in winter than in summer. We don't want a burn to ruin your vacation."

I might've pressed the point, but there would be time

enough to deal with our new reality when we went home. For the moment, there was a warm breeze blowing across one of the prettiest stretches of sand The Good Lord created. Island music wafted around us. Waves lapped at the beach near my toes, I was sipping a painkiller, a pineapple juice and rum concoction I'd developed a fondness for, and all the people I loved best in the world were here.

"I just slathered some on not an hour ago." I stood and stretched, then raised my voice so Mamma, Daddy, Merry, Joe, Poppy, and Blake could hear me. "Anyone need a refill?"

"I'd like some more of my fruit punch, please," said Mamma.

I opened the cooler and reached for her pitcher of painkillers, which was identical to mine, I was reasonably certain. But since she'd asked for very mild drinks, mostly juice, my husband had accommodated her with her own batch. Mamma didn't care much for liquor. That was her story anyway, and we all humored her. Nate was spoiling us all silly. "Here you go, Mamma." I filled her insulated tumbler.

A wild donkey brayed nearby.

I jolted and looked over my shoulder. There are, by some counts, around two hundred wild donkeys on the island of St. John. They roam the island, most often around Coral Bay, the East End, and the North Shore beaches. The donkeys are generally gentle and harmless.

Two donkeys hovered nearby, while a third tried to open one of our coolers with his mouth.

"Lookee there. He wants a beer," said Daddy. "Hey, buddy. I'll help you out." He stood and walked towards the cooler.

Nate beat him there. "Frank, beer's not good for the donkeys."

"How 'bout I give him a treat?" asked Daddy.

"The thing is, when people feed them, they don't have to forage for food. Then they forget how, start depending on people. Then comes the slow season, or, a storm, and the donkeys have forgotten how to fend for themselves."

Daddy patted the donkey on the nose. "Sorry, buddy."

"*Frank*," said Mamma. "Leave that creature alone. If he has any sense at all, he'll bite you."

"He's not going to bite me, are you, fella?"

The donkey brayed in answer.

Daddy patted him again, then moved back to his chair.

The donkey followed and sprawled on the sand behind Daddy's recliner. His two friends settled in beside him.

Chuckling, Blake stood to take a picture. "Dad, the donkeys seem to be drawn to you for some reason. You reckon they think you're a kindred spirit?"

Mamma quirked an eyebrow. "You know, there are a great many things I could say about that. But it's nearly

Christmas, and in the spirit of family harmony, I will refrain from comment."

Poppy said, "We just got the reindeer back to the petting zoo, and now the donkeys are following you."

The reindeer Daddy rented to complete his Santa costume for the annual boat parade on Stella Maris had led us on a merry chase—but that was a whole nother story.

"Y'all are just jealous the donkeys don't want to sit by you," said Daddy.

"Thank Heaven for mercies big and small," said Mamma.

"Oh how adorable! Y'all don't mind if we pet them, do you?" Two ladies of Mamma's generation, or there-abouts, and by the familiar cadence and tone of their voices, from our part of the world, or thereabouts, approached from down the beach.

"Well, they don't belong to us," said Mamma. "Help yourselves. Where are y'all from?"

"We're from Greenville, South Carolina," said the brunette. "I'm Beverly Baker. Actually, I live in Twins-burg, Ohio now. We have an annual Twins Days Festival? Maybe you've heard of it. But I'm originally from the Upstate. This is my dear friend, Frankie Summey." Frankie was approximately the same height as her friend—both were petite. But Frankie was a blonde who wore her hair a bit shorter than Beverly's chin-length style.

"My goodness, what a small world!" said Mamma.

"We're from Stella Maris, near Charleston. I'm Carolyn Talbot. This is my husband, Frank, and our children Blake, Liz, and Merry. That's Blake's wife Poppy over there—she's expecting our first grandchild—Liz's husband, Nate, and Merry's husband, Joe. And this exceptionally helpful young man is Bartholomew."

We all said hey, pleased to meet you, and so forth.

"I just can't believe y'all are from Greenville," Mamma said. "I've got cousins all over Greenville, some of them removed once or twice. My maiden name was Moore. Do y'all know any Moores? Some of my people are Underwoods."

Beverly said, "I know some Underwoods who run a hardware store."

"That's not them," said Mamma. They're all in the automotive industry."

"I'd like to get a picture with the donkeys," said Frankie.

"Here, I'll take one for you." Nate reached for her phone.

Beverly and Frankie posed near the donkeys, but not too near. Then they waved Mamma over. She hesitated at first, then, perhaps due to the calming nature of the painkillers, she slid over beside Beverly.

"Nate, get a picture of us with your camera too, would you, Darlin'?" asked Mamma.

"Sure thing," said Nate.

After they'd finished their photo shoot, Mamma said,

"Liz, Honey, do we have any more tumblers?"

"Sure," I said. "Would y'all like a painkiller?"

"Oh, that sounds wonderful," said Beverly.

Frankie smiled and said, "Yes, please."

By the time I'd reached the cooler, Nate was already pouring them.

"Relax, Slugger," he said. "I've got this." He walked towards Mamma and her new friends, who were spreading towels in the sand by Mamma's chair.

Beverly and Frankie made themselves at home, and chattered away with Mamma like they'd known each other forever. Merry and Poppy went back to reading. Everyone else went back to basking in the sun.

Nate and I settled back in our chairs. "Those three are cut from the same cloth," said Nate.

"That's a fact." I watched them for a few minutes. With the breeze and the surf, I couldn't make out everything they were saying, but I could hear them going on about a recipe for she crab soup. Beverly, apparently, was some sort of food-related blogger ... maybe a restaurant reviewer. She and Mamma could talk food for days, no doubt. I closed my eyes and drifted off.

I was partway asleep, teetering on the edge of beach-induced dream-state, when I noticed their tones had changed. Something was off. I opened an eye and squinted in their direction.

Mamma, Beverly, and Frankie had their heads together. The look on Mamma's face was one I knew well.

It was the one that said there was something she was *not* going to have. I climbed out of my chair and went to see what was going on. Colleen hopped out of her hammock and joined me. No one can actually see Colleen except Nate and me, unless she solidifies, which she does as the situation calls for it. We're her sole human points of contact.

"Everything all right, Mamma?" I asked.

"Liz, Sugar, do you think it would be possible for us to give Beverly and Frankie a ride back to their hotel? A taxi dropped them off here this morning."

I knew there was more to the story, even then, just based on Mamma's countenance. But I couldn't see what harm it would do. "I'm sure it will be fine. Is there anyone else in your party?"

A worried look crossed Beverly's face. "No, no ... just the two of us."

Frankie stared down the beach as if looking for someone. Beverly and Frankie exchanged a look I couldn't read.

"We've got four Jeeps here," I said. "There's plenty of room. Y'all are welcome to ride with Nate and me. We'll drop you. Bartholomew can get everyone else back to the house."

Mamma smiled, an expression on her face that let me know she endorsed this plan.

"Oh, are you sure it's not too much trouble?" Beverly looked relieved.

"Of course not."

"Thank you so much," said Beverly. "We really do appreciate that."

"No worries," I said. "Where are you staying?"

"At the Westin," said Beverly.

A decidedly worried expression settled onto Colleen's face.

I cast her a look with a question.

"I can't intervene here," she said, then added mysteriously, "not yet, anyway."

Exactly what can you not intervene in? What's going on here? I threw the thought at her.

"If I tell you, and you do anything at all differently because of that knowledge, then I've intervened. I repeat. I cannot intervene."

There are rules about what Colleen can get involved in as a guardian spirit, which is a whole nother thing from a ghost. She's not a ghost, just ask her. She's passed on and been sent back with a mission. Recently, she was put in time-out for operating outside that mission, something I'll forever be deeply grateful for. She saved Nate's life, something that was beyond the scope of her assignment. I know she doesn't regret that, but she crossed a line, and she's definitely on good behavior, for the time being, anyway.

To this day, I wonder if my impulse to help that afternoon on Trunk Bay—and to please Mamma—was outside *my* mission, and maybe sent us down a path that might've been avoided.

Chapter Two

The first unusual thing that happened that afternoon after we'd dropped Beverly and Frankie off at the Westin and made our way back up the hill to Cinnamon Ridge was that Mamma changed her mind, something that happens only slightly more frequently than waterspouts over Death Valley.

She lounged in the shade of a covered porch, taking in the gorgeous views of Jost Van Dyke across a narrow channel of the Atlantic.

"Thank you for dropping off Beverly and Frankie," she said to Nate and me as we wandered out onto the porch.

"Our pleasure," said Nate.

"This view is just stunning." Mamma sighed, gave a wistful look, as if the view somehow troubled her.

"Mamma?" I looked at her sideways. "What's up?"

"Well, I was just thinking, for the first time, I really wish I had one of those phones you all have that take such pretty pictures. I'd love to take a photo of this beautiful view and send it to Grace."

For years we'd tried to convince Mamma to carry an iPhone. It would've made all of our lives easier if we could've reached out and touched her a little more reliably. Up until that moment, she'd been steadfast in her resistance. She carried one of the first flip phones ever made in case of emergency. But she never turned the thing on unless she wanted to place a call, so it was useless for the rest of us as a means to get ahold of her.

Nate and I exchanged a look. I might've sent a telepathic message to my husband that said, *Quick, let's get her one before she changes her mind.*

"Well, Carolyn," said Nate, "I believe we're in luck. If memory serves, there's a Radio Shack on St. Thomas that sells iPhones. Why don't I pop over there right quick?"

"Oh, I don't want to be any trouble," said Mamma.

"No trouble at all," said Nate.

The second unusual thing happened while Nate took the boat he'd rented and moored at Cruz Bay over to St. Thomas to get the requested device.

I'd taken a seat on the lounge chair beside Mamma to enjoy the vista before us. The countless shades of blue in the water and sky, the vibrant greens of the dense foliage covering the islands scattered across the water, and the pop of colorful sails in the wind was almost too beautiful to be real.

"I could stare at this all day," I said.

"Oh, I could too," said Mamma. "What are our plans for dinner?"

There was something in her voice I should've caught, but didn't. "Nate made reservations at The Lime Inn. They have a six-course tasting menu he thought would be fun."

"That does sound scrumptious," said Mamma. "But you know, I was looking at all the restaurant menus in that binder in the living room?"

"Right..."

"And I have an absolute hankering for that coconut panko encrusted grouper at Jolly Mon Grill. Have you ever had that?"

"I have, actually. I had it when we were here on our honeymoon, and it is delicious."

"Do you suppose we could go there tonight? Maybe have the tasting menu another night?" asked Mamma.

"Mamma, I seriously doubt we can get a reservation on this short of notice. This is the busy season here..."

"Well, could we try? I mean, I hate to be any trouble at all. Nate has been just so, so generous bringing us all here. We'll never be able to thank him enough. I can't even imagine how much all this is costing. Y'all should let us pay for some of this. Seriously, now. It's just not—"

"Mamma, that's not necessary at all, really." This was

not a path I wanted to go down with her. And I had a feeling we would be having this conversation many times over the two weeks we were here. "Why don't I just call Jolly Mon Grill and see if they can work us in?"

"Oh, would you, Sugar?" Mamma smiled a big, happy smile. "Thank you so much. You are so sweet to your old mamma. I just can't get that grouper out of my mind."

"Well, I'll give it a try." I felt my eyebrows slide up my forehead. I was highly skeptical I'd be able to pull this off.

But as it turned out, Jolly Mon Grill had a cancellation, and could take us at eight o'clock, which fit our schedule perfectly. By the time we were heading for the Jeeps, Mamma had her new iPhone, and Nate had shown her how to take pictures and send text messages. My husband has an abundance of patience.

"Everybody stand in front of the house," said Mamma. "Let me take your picture."

We humored Mamma, as was our custom. We all gathered in the middle of the walkway that extended the length of the house. Supported by columns made from distinctive St. John stonework with embedded shells, the pergola was surrounded by all manner of palms and exotic greenery.

"Now, Miss Carolyn," said Bartholomew, "you need to be in the picture yourself. Why don't you give me your phone, and I'll take the picture for you?"

Mamma favored him with a sunny smile. "Aren't you

the sweetest thing? Thank you, Bartholomew. I can't wait for Grace to see this house."

We made room for her, and she slid in beside Daddy. Colleen put one arm around my shoulder and one around Nate's, and stuck her head between ours. I doubted we'd be able to see her in the photo, but we'd always know she was in it. Bartholomew snapped the picture, then we all piled in the Jeeps and headed into Cruz Bay.

Some detective I am. I confess I had a vague notion Mamma was up to something. But never in my wildest dreams did I imagine what.

Chapter Three

There are two towns in St. John. Cruz Bay on the west side of the island, facing St. Thomas, is where the ferries dock. Most of the shops and restaurants are in Cruz Bay. Coral Bay is all the way across the island, and while there are some restaurants and a handful of shops, it's more geared to people who live in St. John year-round and somewhat less tourist focused. You will see literal live chickens crossing the street in both places, any day of the week. It's that kind of island. Nate and I love it, but I had concerns about my parents, and whether it was really their speed. So far, they both seemed to be having a great time. I was especially happy that Mamma seemed to be letting her hair down a little.

Jolly Mon Grill was a Caribbean restaurant in Cruz Bay across from the National Park dock with a casual, breezy, and yet still somehow elegant ambience. As far as I could tell, most of the dining room was actually a large covered deck with multiple levels, stonework planters, and occasional lattice screens that suggested walls. Ceiling fans swirled the air and caressed the fronds and leaves of countless potted plants that blended with the palm trees and tropical foliage surrounding the place. Oil paintings with a beachy, impressionist vibe hung on the lattice. Comfortable, dark wicker armchairs complemented tables with white cloths. Combined with all the other elements, the hefty dark-stained support posts suggested a more substantial structure. But like many restaurants in St. John, it was a very nice covered deck attached to a building that housed a kitchen, storage, and all such as that. Our table that night was situated on a level a few steps up from the main floor.

Savory smells of seafood and steaks on a grill wafted through the restaurant. Soft steel drum music floated around us. I smiled as I noticed Merry swaying to the beat just as I was. It was a magical evening. Everyone was smiling, laughing, having a good time.

Our waiter patiently described three cocktails to Mamma before she decided on a Mango Tango, a frozen concoction with vodka and two kinds of rum. Daddy raised his eyebrows but didn't say a word, which was so far out of character for him I nearly opened my mouth to comment. Daddy's favorite sport was aggravating Mamma. It wasn't like him to let such an opportunity pass.

"Hush up." Colleen perched on the railing near the head of the table.

That was something I frequently said to her. *What?* I scrunched my face at her.

"It was all I could do to keep him quiet," she said. "Leave well enough alone."

I ordered a pomegranate martini, Nate a Woodford Reserve on the rocks. Our waiter suggested a virgin mango colada for Poppy. After everyone else chose from the menu of creative cocktails and the drinks had been delivered, Blake tapped his margarita glass.

"Here's to Nate," he said. "Thank you for this amazing trip. I can't even imagine all the work that went into planning this. I won't be vulgar and mention how much it must be costing. But I know it's too much. To our host."

"To Nate," we all chimed in.

"Dinner's on me tonight," said Daddy.

"Thank you, Frank," said Nate. "That's an awfully kind offer, but it's already been taken care of. Please enjoy your dinner."

Daddy screwed up his face. "How does that work? We haven't even ordered yet."

"Daddy please," I said. "Let it go." No doubt Nate had given the manager a credit card when we came in to ward off just such an effort.

"Franklin." Mamma's tone held an admonishment.

He shrugged, shook his head, and opened his menu.

"How about I order a few appetizers for the table?" asked Nate. "What looks good to everyone?"

"Maybe some calamari?" said Blake.

"I love the snapper ceviche," I said.

"I'd like to try that," said Merry.

"How about the empanadas?" said Poppy. "I need to watch how much seafood I'm having, and I overheard the waiter telling the next table they're beef today."

"Yes, indeed," said Mamma. "You need to be careful about that."

"You hear that?" Daddy grinned. "My grandson needs some beef. Tomorrow, I expect he'll want some more of that fine brisket we had."

"You're sure it's not a granddaughter, are you?" Poppy smiled, gave him a teasing look.

"I'm happy either way," said Daddy. "Just get me a healthy grandbaby. But I suspect it's a boy."

In the end, Nate ordered some of all the appetizers mentioned, plus some grilled shrimp. For the next few minutes, we chattered happily about our entree selections. When I'd decided on the creamy seafood paella, I laid my menu on the table and took a sip of my martini.

Mamma was seated to my left. Her menu was on the table, and she fiddled with her new phone.

"You still feeling like the grouper?" I asked.

"Oh my yes," she said. "I've been thinking about it all afternoon." She lifted her phone and tapped the button to take a photo, I assumed of Merry, Joe, and Poppy, who sat across the table.

"Why don't we ask the waiter to take one of all of us?" I asked.

"That's a good idea." She looked a little distracted and kept snapping pictures.

"We might need to take that thing away from you," I teased.

She gave me a look that informed me she'd like to see me try that.

I took another sip of my drink.

As soon as the waiter had taken our dinner orders, Mamma said, "I need to run powder my nose."

"I'll come with you." I started to stand.

"No need," said Mamma. "You just sit right there and enjoy your drink. I'm still capable of going to the ladies' room by myself. I'm not feeble yet."

"Hell's bells, Mamma ... I didn't mean *that* at all." I squinted at her. We often went to the ladies' room together in restaurants. What was up with her this evening?

"*Elizabeth.* Language. I'll be right back," she said to me as she stood. "Excuse me," she said in a louder voice.

Merry said, "I'll come—"

"Sit still." Mamma gave her a smile and a look that did not invite discussion.

Merry wrinkled her nose at me.

I shrugged.

Nate and Joe were talking about our planned day sail to Jost Van Dyke the next day.

"I'd planned for us to have lunch at White Bay, maybe at Hendo's Hideout. Would you rather go to Foxy's?" He looked at me.

"I love Foxy's," I said, "but Hendo's is more convenient if we're spending the day at White Bay."

Nate shrugged. "No reason we can't hit Foxy's first."

We all discussed the pros and cons of the various options for lunch the next day for a few minutes, until two servers arrived with our appetizers. They put them all in the middle of the table, and we oohed and ahhed over them.

I caught Daddy scanning the restaurant for Mamma. My eyes followed his as he found her. "What in the devil is she doing?"

"She's having fun with her new phone," I said. "Taking pictures of the restaurant to send to Grace."

Daddy shook his head. "Might shouldn't a got her one of those."

Mamma made her way back to the table, and we all dug into the appetizers. For a while, we focused on the bounty of fresh seafood and the flaky empanadas in front of us. Everything was delicious. Anyone watching might've thought we hadn't eaten in a while, the way we scarfed everything down.

A server arrived with a fresh round of drinks, and to my astonishment, Mamma didn't object. She picked up her fresh glass, smiled at the server, and put the straw in her mouth. That was the first time I can ever recall Mamma having multiple mixed drinks at a meal—and she'd had painkillers on the beach that afternoon. This was completely out of character, but we were on vacation, and I was happy she was relaxing.

The appetizer plates were cleared and our entrees delivered. Everyone prattled happily about the amazing food, our day at Trunk Bay, tomorrow's trip to Jost Van Dyke, and our plans for Christmas Day. Colleen entertained herself by chatting up Bartholomew, who of course could not hear her. He did seem to sense her presence, in much the same way my godmother, Grace, sometimes did. Colleen waved a hand in front of his face, snapped her fingers at him, and generally did her best to get his attention. For his part, Bartholomew looked uneasy.

Stop tormenting him. I threw the thought at her. *You're distracting him from his job.*

"Do you seriously—" Colleen stopped mid-sentence, an odd look on her face. She scanned the restaurant, then rolled her eyes at me. But she didn't mess with Bartholomew again.

As I delivered a bite of creamy paella to my mouth, I glanced at Mamma. Staring at something behind Blake's head, she set her fork down on her plate and picked up her phone. I followed her gaze.

A man probably of Mamma and Daddy's generation rose from a table across the room and headed towards the restrooms. A young blonde woman, probably in her early to mid-twenties, remained by herself at the table.

"Do you know those folks?" I asked Mamma.

She jumped a little bit. "Of course not." She picked up her fork. "This grouper is out of this world. Would you like a bite?"

"No thank you," I said. "I won't be able to finish my paella."

Mamma seemed focused on her plate. Maybe she'd just been daydreaming. I glanced back to the table she'd been watching. One of the bartenders approached the young woman and leaned down to talk to her. After a few minutes, he put a hand on her arm in a very familiar way. She jerked it away from him, said something, her expression angry.

He glanced over his shoulder and apparently saw the older gentleman, who was headed back to the table. The bartender spoke to the blonde again, then walked back to the bar.

The older gentleman wore an angry, questioning look. He addressed the blonde, gestured towards the bartender.

"Oh dear," Mamma said.

I turned to her. She was snapping pictures.

"*Mamma?*" I said. "What in this world are you doing?"

By this time, Daddy and Nate were watching the action across the room, where the older gentleman strode towards the bar.

The bartender headed towards the kitchen.

The older gentleman followed him.

The blonde followed the older gentleman.

Mamma kept taking pictures.

After a few moments, the young blonde woman returned to the table. She stared in the direction of the kitchen, as if she had expected her dinner companion to follow her. Presently, he did, an odd look on his face. What looked like an argument ensued. She put a hand on his arm and stroked it a bit. Then she leaned in and kissed him on the cheek.

"Huzzy." Mamma had always preferred the 'z' variation of this term of disapproval. Somehow it sounded far more disgraceful than 'hussy' rolling from her lips.

"Carolyn?" Daddy stared at Mamma.

The rest of us cast her questioning glances.

She smiled, laid down her phone. "I believe this is the best grouper I've had in my life. Did anyone else order it?"

We all continued to stare at her.

"What?" she asked, then picked up her fork and delivered a bite of fish to her mouth, an angelic look on her face.

"Who are those people?" asked Daddy.

Mamma gave a little shrug. "I've never met them. Have you?"

"No," said Daddy. "But I'd like to know why you were taking their picture."

"Don't be ridiculous, Frank. How was your ribeye?"

asked Mamma. "You must've enjoyed it. You've cleaned your plate. And you didn't mention once how you couldn't take scraps home to Chumley. Do you suppose we should try Moon Unit after dinner?"

"Mamma?" I looked at her. "What are you up to?"

Her expression was the picture of innocence. "What? Well, it's just clear that gentleman is having dinner with a young lady less than half his age. I was just thinking it's sad. The old fool probably has a family somewhere that's missing him at Christmas. And she ... well, it must be getting close to that child's bedtime."

"Maybe it's her father," said Merry.

"Hmmpf." Mamma scoffed. "And maybe I'm a Rockette."

"Those are consenting adults, and this is none of our business," said Blake.

Bartholomew wore a slight grin. He looked at Mamma like maybe he was thinking he was on to her. "Miss Carolyn, where were your new friends having dinner this evening?"

"My new friends?" She smiled at him, tilted her head.

"Yeah, you know ... the ladies you met on the beach this afternoon. What were their names again?"

"Oh, you mean Beverly and Frankie," said Mamma.

"Yeah, that's right."

"I don't know if they mentioned where they were headed," said Mamma. "Is anyone else interested in dessert? I can't stop thinking about that key lime pie. It's got white chocolate mousse on top. Doesn't that sound divine?"

A look passed between Nate and Bartholomew.

"I'll have a bite of that," said Merry.

"It sounds dangerous," said Poppy. "But I'd like a slice."

We ordered one each of all the other desserts—and three slices of the key lime pie with white chocolate mousse. Mamma's eye occasionally traveled to the table with the May–December couple while we devoured the decadent treats, but Poppy launched into a subject near and dear to Mamma's heart—decorating the nursery—and that kept her occupied.

The couple in question left the restaurant a few moments before us. As we walked back to the Jeeps, which we'd parked in a paid lot on King Street, there they were on the sidewalk right ahead of us. When we came to Aunt Odella's Famous Brisket stand, Colleen crossed the street to the bright pink and green painted lean-to.

"If your mamma recommends these biscuits, I need to try one," said Colleen. "Get me two with the brisket."

We just ate, for goodness' sake. How am I going to explain buying biscuits now?

Colleen laughed her distinctive bray-snort laugh, "I promise you, you won't be the only one placing an order."

I shook my head and followed Colleen across the street, holding up a finger and calling, "Give me a sec." I got in line acting innocent, like this was perfectly normal behavior.

"Liz?" Nate's single syllable carried the question, *What in the name of sweet reason are you doing?*

I offered him my sunniest smile.

"Oh heck yeah." Blake followed me across the street, and the rest of the group straggled behind him. "Let's get a couple dozen to keep in the refrigerator. I could eat these every day."

When our turn came, Aunt Odella herself once again took our order. "Well, it's good t' see you all again." Her wide smile radiated warmth. If I had to guess, I'd've placed her in her midsixties. A headful of dreadlocks swept below her shoulders. The tie-dyed T-shirt and shorts she wore must've been the uniform for the business. The cook manning the smoker in the back wore an identical set.

"We can't seem to get enough of your brisket and biscuits," I said. "I'd like three dozen, please."

"With slaw and pickle?" She was unfazed by the number.

"Yes, please," I said.

"Could we possibly get extra pickles?" asked Poppy.

"Why sure you can," said Aunt Odella.

"Darlin' Poppy is expecting our first grandchild." Mamma edged in front of me. "In June. They'll be moving into a new house soon, and of course we're planning the nursery."

"Grandchildren are God's sweetest blessings." Aunt Odella placed a hand on her chest. "I have three myself."

Mamma and Aunt Odella carried on about cribs and bumpers and all such as that until the customers behind us started showing signs of restlessness. We paid for our order and moved over to wait at the end of the building.

"Unbelievable." Mamma stared up North Shore Road.

We all turned to see what she was talking about.

Three donkeys moseyed down the center of the street.

"There they are." Daddy sounded positively gleeful.

"Oh my stars," I said. "They don't usually come into Cruz Bay."

"They're looking for their leader," said Mamma.

"Won't they get hit by a car?" Merry asked. "This is dangerous. We need to get them out of the road."

"They'll be fine," said Nate. "People here are used to them."

We stared in disbelief as the donkeys sauntered over to where we were standing and sidled up to Daddy.

"Frank, you need to shoo those things away," said Mamma. "They could be carrying some disease for all we know."

"It's not like they're trained, Carolyn. They're not going to do what I tell them."

"Could you at least *try?*" Mamma's voice held a smidge of panic. "We can't risk exposing Poppy to the donkey flu."

Daddy looked troubled. He spoke to Blake. "Take Poppy back to the other side of the street, why don't you?"

Blake glanced at Nate.

"Maybe everyone should go back across the street," said Nate. "I'll wait for the food."

"That's a good idea." He swept his right arm in an after you gesture. Everyone except Nate and Daddy crossed the street.

This gave the donkeys unfettered access to Daddy, and they moved closer, surrounding him. He spoke to them in low, soothing tones, but I couldn't make out what he was saying.

"Well, it's official," said Mamma. "He's the jackass whisperer."

Nate collected our food and joined us. Daddy said his goodbyes, stepped around the donkeys, and moved quickly to our side of the street.

As we moved through the intersection at the corner, North Shore Road became King Street. Mamma set the pace, and we walked faster than we generally did as a group on an after-dinner stroll. The donkeys ambled after us. At the intersection of King and Prince, the couple who'd kept Mamma so occupied during dinner came out of Woody's Saloon, crossed in front of us, and headed down a narrow, one-way leg of Prince Street that was pleasantly shaded in daytime, but shrouded in darkness at night.

I glanced over my shoulder as we entered the intersection. From the shadows, two large figures emerged, one from the left and one on the right. There wasn't a doubt in my mind they'd been lying in wait. The one on the left was unusually tall and brawny. He had a distinctive cat-like walk, like he was maybe on the prowl. The two fell in step behind the couple, something overtly sinister in their movements.

I stopped in the middle of the intersection. "I'm so full from dinner," I said, in a voice louder than necessary. "Do y'all mind if we take the long way back to the cars?"

No one minded, as it turned out, and our loud and unruly group paraded down Prince Street after the couple and the two men behind them. The donkeys brought up the rear. Sometimes all it took to prevent a crime was for there to be an audience. If the odd couple from the restaurant were being targeted by thugs looking to rob them, our presence on the street might be enough to abort it. Or maybe my imagination was running away with me, and the two men who'd appeared from nowhere were just out for an evening stroll.

But a couple of quick glances told me Nate and Bartholomew were both on high alert. They tracked the two men as the couple turned left onto Strand Street, and we all followed. When May and December reached their car in a small lot across from Wharfside Village, the pair of potential thieves stared as they climbed inside. The two men exchanged a glance, then picked up their pace.

At the end of the street, they turned left at a jog. When we reached the corner, they'd disappeared.

"Those two were up to no good," said Bartholomew.

"I was thinking the same thing," said Nate. "And we don't know where they are at the moment. If they missed one opportunity, they may be looking for another."

When we reached the parking lot, the rest of us stood watch while Nate and Bartholomew went over the three Jeeps we'd driven to dinner looking for trackers, tampering, or any sort of mischief. After they were sure the cars hadn't been messed with, we climbed in and made our way back to the house. Nate, Bartholomew, and Blake drove, each taking a slightly different route.

It didn't occur to me until the ride home that if the two men had criminal intent, we could've been the target all along. The thugs could've been circling the block to attack us before we reached the Jeeps. It seemed unlikely, but that was the thing about all of Nate's money. It changed everything.

There were so many things I'd never have to worry about again—like how to pay the taxes on the house, or where to get the money to have it painted. But there was a whole new list of things to be concerned about.

Like who might be plotting to take some of that money for themselves, and what lengths they might go to to get it.

Chapter Four

Christmas Eve dawned clear and bright. Of course it was very different, being in the islands for Christmas. But the tropical setting didn't hamper my excitement one teeny bit. I was positively giddy with Christmas spirit, and excited to celebrate with my family. I wrapped the last of my gifts before anyone else was up and put them under the tree in the family room.

The layout of the house was perfect for our group. It was built into the hillside and comprised of three levels, with the family room, dining area, and kitchen in the center of the main floor, which was the top floor. Nearly the entire north-facing wall that overlooked Cinnamon Bay and the Atlantic Ocean beyond was made of sliding glass doors. We loved keeping the doors open, the deck blending with the living room, the lush hillside beyond a veritable Garden of Eden offering complete privacy. At the top of a hill, the property bordered the National Park. At night, the birds and tree frogs and jungle critters made so much noise it was unsettling at first.

Each of the five bedrooms had a private bath. Two of the suites were at opposite ends of the top level. Nate and I were in the one to the left, and Bartholomew had the one to the right. Downstairs, the lower level of the house was actually the first basement, the back of it set into the hillside, the front open to the same views we had upstairs.

This part of the house was made from thick poured concrete walls that provided virtually soundproof rooms. Mamma and Daddy, Blake and Poppy, and Merry and Joe each had private suites on this level, with Mamma and Daddy closest to the pool deck on the far end, Merry and Joe in the middle, and Blake and Poppy on the opposite end.

All of the bedrooms had breathtaking views of the ocean and the verdant hillside surrounding the house. Each bedroom had its own sliding door to the patio, which wrapped from the pool deck all the way around that level of the house to a gently sloping set of steps outside Blake and Poppy's room that led back to the driveway. Another basement below the guest quarters housed a cistern.

Nate had hired a woman named Jenny to stock the house with groceries, cook for us whenever we wanted to eat in, and make the occasional blender of fruity liquor drinks. When I stumbled into the kitchen that Christmas

Eve morning, she was putting the finishing touches on a breakfast buffet. A delicate, petite Black woman with long black hair, she exuded grace.

"Those cinnamon rolls smell heavenly." I inhaled deeply. My eyes might've rolled back in my head a bit.

"Thank you," she said. "That's my grandma's secret recipe. She claims it's what convinced my grandfather to marry her."

"I wouldn't doubt it," I said. "Maybe I should test one."

She slid one onto a plate and handed it to me. "I think that's for the best. You never know. This batch might not be any good. But save room for the casserole and some fruit. The pineapple is really good today." She smiled shyly.

As I took the plate, I admired the tattoo that ran from the back of her hand all the way up to her shoulder. It was a tree branch with flowers and butterflies. Now, I'm not the tattoo type myself at all. But I recognized beautiful work when I saw it.

I poured myself a cup of coffee and wolfed down the cinnamon roll while we chatted for a few minutes. I knew Jenny was in and out—I saw the results: food ready to eat at exactly the right time, a fresh pitcher of iced tea, the basket of cookies that wasn't there yesterday. But I'd rarely seen her. She was highly efficient and nearly invisible.

"This may be the best cinnamon roll I've ever eaten," I said. "But shhh—don't let my mamma hear me say that."

"She's out on the deck." Jenny smiled. "I think you're good."

I polished off the cinnamon roll. "I'm going to finish my coffee and wait for everyone else for the rest of my breakfast. Thank you so much for doing all of this."

"I'm happy you like my cooking." She pulled a card from her back pocket. "Nate knows how to reach me, of course. But if you're ever coming down by yourself and need anything, just call."

"I'll do that, thanks." I started to lay the card on the bar, then spied my laptop backpack, which I'd left on one of the barstools the day we arrived. I needed to put that away. "You never know when we might need a girls' trip."

I took my coffee out to the deck and settled into a lounger beside Mamma.

"I was going to make pancakes," she said, "but someone's already made breakfast. Did you do all that?"

I grinned at her. "No, I didn't cook." I explained about Jenny. "Did you not see her in the kitchen?"

"No," said Mamma. "No one was there when I came upstairs."

I shrugged. "She's really good at being unobtrusive. Some days the breakfast menu is simple, like the muffins and bagels and fruit and all from the past couple of days. Other days are like what she's got going on in there this morning. Have you eaten? That breakfast casserole looks like one of yours."

"Not yet. I'm going to finish my coffee first. Did Jenny

decorate the house for Christmas too? That tree is just stunning. I'd like to have a few of the beachy-looking ornaments as a memento. Is there a local shop where we can buy those?"

"Several places, yes. We'll definitely be doing some shopping. And yes, Jenny decorated the tree and put up the greenery and candles and all indoors, though I think someone else strung all those little white lights on the house and the palm trees."

"She's a wonder, that Jenny," said Mamma. "I'd like to take her home with me. Sugar … what do we have planned for today? Sailing, did you say?"

"Yes, Nate arranged a private charter over to Jost Van Dyke—that island right there." I pointed across the water. "There's a beautiful beach, and several places for lunch. But the sailing is the best part I think."

"That does sound fun…" Her tone alerted me that she was thinking the opposite of what she said.

"What's wrong, Mamma? You've always liked to sail."

"That's true," said Mamma. "I was just thinking it might be fun to explore St. John a bit more. We've barely seen *this* island."

"Oh, we're going to, trust me. We're going to see every nook and cranny of St. John."

"I think your Daddy wanted to take one of the Jeeps and just knock around a bit. Would that be all right? Could we go sailing a different day? Maybe he could take me shopping for Christmas ornaments."

"You mean just the two of you?" The idea of them going off by themselves alarmed me more than it would've a week ago. My parents were neither feeble nor prone to getting lost. But St. John was unfamiliar territory to them, and the hilly roads full of hairpin turns with steep drop-offs. Then there was the whole thing with the money, and them not knowing we were all at an increased risk for being taken hostage, extortion, fraud, and a multitude of financial crimes I'd never even heard of. Was it irresponsible not to tell them?

"Well, yes, just the two of us," said Mamma. "I'm sure you and Nate would like some time alone. The rest of us can entertain ourselves for a while. You're celebrating your anniversary for goodness' sake."

"Hmmm."

"You didn't mean for us to spend every second of two whole weeks together, did you?"

"I think Nate did, actually," I said. "He's made a lot of plans..." He'd gone to a lot of trouble to make everything perfect. It hadn't occurred to me anyone would have their own plans. Suddenly, I felt very selfish.

"Oh no." Mamma wore a sick look. "I didn't mean to sound ungrateful at all. I'm terribly sorry. Whatever you all have planned is fine with me, of course." She twisted her hands together and generally looked flustered, which is quite unusual for Mamma. Something was going on with her. Something beyond a desire to shop for Christmas ornaments.

"Mamma?" I gave her a long, inquiring look.

She huffed a sigh. "I'm terrible at this."

"At what?"

"I suppose I'll have to tell you. Is Nate up?"

"He went for a swim just before I came out here. What is going on with you?" I asked.

"Well, let's finish our coffee and wait for Nate."

"Carolyn, is everything all right?" Nate appeared as if summoned, and sat on the end of my lounge chair.

"We don't need to discuss this in front of everyone, all right, Darlin'?" Mamma's look held a plea.

"You can rely on my discretion, of course," said Nate.

She heaved another deep sigh. "I have a confession to make."

We waited.

Mamma set her gaze somewhere on the horizon. "You remember the ladies we met on the beach yesterday? Beverly and Frankie?"

"Yes, of course," I said.

"Well," said Mamma, "that was Beverly's husband last night in the restaurant. With the child date."

"I see," said Nate.

We waited for Mamma to go on.

"The child is a tantrum yoga instructor," said Mamma.

"Tantrum?" I felt my face scrunch. "You mean ... tantra or tantric, maybe?"

"Elizabeth," said Mamma. "Wrinkles."

I smoothed the confused expression off my face.

"No," said Mamma. "Tantrum yoga is apparently exactly what it sounds like. Folks pay to have someone show them how to throw a temper tantrum while they stretch. It's the latest thing, I'm told. Apparently, that's how Melvin—that's Beverly's husband—met the child. In tantrum class. There's a certain symmetry there, I suppose."

"So they're separated, Beverly and her husband? Or are they divorced?" I asked.

"Neither," said Mamma. "He doesn't know that Beverly knows about the affair. And she didn't, until very recently. Their children couldn't make it home for Christmas—they're grown, of course. Beverly had planned a romantic holiday for just the two of them, and then he just leaves. Three days before Christmas."

"What an utter ass," I said.

"He told her he had an emergency business meeting out of town. Melvin owns a *window treatment franchise.* They don't *have* out-of-town mini blind emergencies three days before Christmas. Of course, Beverly knew he was lying. She went through his laptop and found an email receipt for the airline tickets and the hotel. She and Frankie decided to come see for themselves exactly what and who he was doing."

Nate nodded. "They're conducting their own investigation."

"That's right," said Mamma wide-eyed. "Apparently, that sort of thing can be quite expensive."

"It can be," agreed Nate.

"Well, Beverly couldn't take that kind of money from their joint account without explanation, though I don't know how she planned to explain away what this trip cost, actually. I'm not sure she thought this all the way through. Anyway, she and Frankie figured they could get the goods. But as it turns out, mostly they've been hiding in their room because they're afraid Melvin will see them. Yesterday, Melvin and the tantrum tartlet took some sort of day trip to another island."

"Like we're planning to do today, going over to Jost Van Dyke," I said.

"Exactly," said Mamma. "Beverly and Frankie spent the day on the beach. They could hardly follow them onto a boat. Melvin would surely have recognized them in the group."

"And last night?" I raised an eyebrow at Mamma.

"I suppose I got carried away with myself," said Mamma. "You all lead such exciting lives. I guess when Beverly told me what was going on … well, for a minute or two, I thought, 'Well, I can snoop as easily as Elizabeth can. She got that gift from somewhere.' I may have exaggerated to Beverly my knowledge of domestic investigations by proxy."

I nodded. "That's why you needed an iPhone. And that's why you suddenly wanted the grouper at Jolly Mon

Grill. Beverly must've known where they were headed, but she and Frankie didn't dare follow them."

"Exactly," said Mamma. "I figured I could take a few pictures and help them out. How hard could that be?"

"You certainly took plenty of photos," I said. "His presence here over Christmas with a woman that much younger ... well, it's not proof of adultery, but he'll certainly have a hard time explaining himself to a judge."

"And the proof she needs wouldn't be hard to come by," said Nate.

"The thing is..." Mamma reached over and laid a hand on my leg. "I'm very worried about Beverly and Frankie."

"Why's that?" asked Nate.

"I haven't been able to reach them," said Mamma.

"Maybe they've decided to do something fun. Perhaps they've gone to another beach?" Nate suggested.

"We were supposed to speak last night. They were very eager to hear what happened in the restaurant. I'm not experienced with these smart phones. But I did manage to text them with my new number before dinner, and they did respond."

"That's what you're thinking? You want Daddy to drive you over to the Westin to check on them?" My voice climbed.

"Well..." said Mamma. "Yes, actually. Why would that be a problem?"

"It's probably just a signal issue," said Nate. "Depending on who their carrier is, they most likely have spotty service here. I'm sure it's nothing to worry about."

"I wish I could be sure of that," said Mamma. "Something just doesn't feel right."

"I'm a big believer in instinct," said Nate. "Would you like us to go by and check on them?"

"Oh, would you?" asked Mamma. "I would appreciate that more than I can tell you."

"Sure," said Nate. "We can pop by the Westin before we head to Cruz Bay. Our charter to Jost Van Dyke is a private one, so they won't leave without us."

"That would just set my mind at ease," said Mamma.

"We can't have you stressed," said Nate. "No worries allowed on a sailboat. It's a nautical rule."

"Perhaps I could come along?" said Mamma.

"What's that? Ah..." Nate scratched a spot over his ear. "Carolyn ... I would just feel better about the whole thing if you and Frank rode with Bartholomew and met us at Cruz Bay."

"Morning, everybody." Blake walked onto the deck, followed by Merry and Joe. "Hey, listen, I'm thinking Poppy and I better hang out here today. She's not feeling her sea legs. With the pregnancy ... some days she's completely fine, but others she gets a little queasy. The trip over on the car ferry was rough for her. We'd best stick to dry land."

"Oh no," I said. "Why don't we reschedule for another day?" I looked at Nate.

"Absolutely," he said. "Let's go when she's feeling better."

"Honestly, there's no guarantee she'll be up to it later," said Blake. "Y'all go on ahead. We'll be fine here. We'll chill by the pool."

"A pool day sounds perfect to me," I said.

"It's settled, then," said Nate.

We argued further for a few minutes, everyone trying to make everything perfect for everyone else, because that's what we do.

"Who does a body talk to about coffee in this establishment?" Daddy said.

We turned to see him standing in the kitchen, studying things like a carpenter who'd wandered into a nuclear physics laboratory.

Mamma raised an eyebrow. "The same person who brings you your coffee every morning of your life."

"Oh, that's good news," he said. "She knows how I like it." He turned up the Christmas music and settled in at the dining table. "The First Noel" by Lady A floated through the house and out onto the deck.

Merry and I exchanged a look and shook our heads.

"Don't start, girls," said Mamma. "At his age, he's unlikely to change. And there are far worse things he could be doing."

. . .

I knew she was thinking about Beverly's husband and his extramarital escapade. But I couldn't see Daddy being tempted by a yoga instructor, or a younger woman of any occupation or description for that matter. My daddy was used to a certain level of attention. He worked Mamma's nerves—as a hobby—but he knew how good he had it. He was no fool.

Then again, Beverly and Melvin Baker's children probably thought their parents' marriage was solid too.

After breakfast, which we demolished, including half of the brisket biscuits from Aunt Odella's, after we'd licked the cinnamon roll pan clean, Mamma shooed Nate and me out of the kitchen. "I've got this," she said. "You children go enjoy the island."

She didn't say, "Hurry on out of here and go check on my friends before I dissolve into a nervous wreck."

But we knew exactly what she meant.

Chapter Five

Zipping across St. John, the two of us alone in a Jeep for the first time since we'd arrived, I let go of a breath I didn't realize I'd been holding. This was a dream vacation, all of us traveling together. But I was so anxious for everyone to have a good time I think maybe I'd put myself on twenty-four seven hostess duty. The warm sunshine and the soft island breeze soothed all my tension away. Except the one thing that wouldn't stop nagging at me.

Nate found my hand and gave it a squeeze. "What's on your mind, Slugger?"

"What has my mamma gotten herself into?"

"Nothing we can't get her out of."

And that's one of the things I loved best about my husband. Nate stayed calm—almost never got rattled. He was strong in ways I wasn't. And that strength was worth more to me than any amount of money.

I let the rest of my worry float away and soaked up the beauty all around us. We crested a hill, the verdant shades of green of the forest, dotted here and there with pops of yellow, pink, and white flowers giving way below to the vibrant blues of the ocean stretching out on the horizon. The view was surreal.

St. John is a volcanic island, part of an undersea mountain range that extends from Cuba to Trinidad. Perhaps because of the way the island was formed, it has a craggy, irregular shape, and is surrounded by countless bays. The Westin property takes up most of Great Cruz Bay, which is situated slightly south of Cruz Bay.

We arrived just after ten a.m. We didn't have a room number for Beverly and Frankie, and they didn't answer the phone when we tried calling through the front desk. Mamma had said they were mostly sticking to their room, so we were thinking maybe they were afraid to answer the phone, perhaps fearing Melvin had spotted them and was calling to confirm his suspicions.

While I perched on a sofa on the other side of the lobby pretending to study something critically important on my phone, Nate took the basket of Christmas cookies Jenny had left for us, but miraculously, no one had been into yet, and prevailed upon the young woman at the front desk to make sure they were personally delivered to his Aunt Beverly. He smiled, leaned in to speak to her, and generally hit her with a double-barreled charm offensive. Charm is my husband's superpower.

She checked something in the computer, spoke to her coworker, then picked up the basket and smiled and waved at Nate as she headed off to hand-deliver it herself. Continuing to pretend a preoccupation with my phone, I followed.

Then a text message landed from Mamma:

> Elizabeth, your daddy stood out on the porch and brayed like a deranged Doctor Doolittle till he rounded himself up a donkey. Three donkeys. Possibly the same three we saw on the beach yesterday. Bartholomew apparently thought it was funny. He doesn't know your daddy well enough to realize how quickly this could prove disastrous.

I needed to talk to Mamma about how texting was generally a briefer form of communication. And I had no doubt Bart could handle whatever nonsense Daddy got into while we were out.

The Westin St. John is a cluster of two-story, cream-colored buildings with blue metal roofs, each with a dozen or so rooms, arranged around a massive beachfront swimming pool. A slew of larger timeshare buildings were scattered up the hill and around the perimeter. The clerk with the basket made her way along the brick path, through the meticulously landscaped grounds to the building on the far left, closest to the bay. I stayed far enough behind her so as not to arouse suspicion.

She knocked on the door of a room in the middle of the first floor and waited several minutes. Then she repeated the process. When no one appeared, she hurried down the hall and out the door. I made note of the room number and texted Nate:

> They didn't come to the door. Meet me by the pool?

NATE:

Roger that

The pool was one of the biggest I've seen. Its shape reminds me of an airplane made from children's building blocks. Oversized planters with palm trees were situated in the middle. The irregular shape of the pool and the luxuriant landscaping offered relative privacy in the occasional nook. Nate and I settled into lounge chairs near a group of hibiscus bushes under a palm tree. Having dressed for a day of sailing and shell collecting, we fit right in.

"What are you thinking here?" asked Nate.

"Mamma won't be satisfied with anything less than us laying eyes on them and verifying their safety," I said.

"Well, I know that," said Nate. "I meant where do you suppose they've gotten to?"

I pondered that for a moment. "I think they're in the room and just not answering the door or the phone. All those rooms have sliding glass doors that open onto a patio. Maybe one of us should just knock on the patio door. They can pull back the curtain and see who it is. They wouldn't open the door for a stranger—even one bearing cookies. But they might open it for us."

"That seems simple enough. The other one of us can knock on the door off the hallway."

"Then again, that might scare them." I said. "They might feel—"

"*Psst.*"

Nate and I looked at each other.

"*Pssssst.*"

Something rustled in the bushes behind us.

"Beverly?" I called softly.

"It's me—us," came the reply. "I guess Carolyn must've told you what was going on."

"Why are you in the bushes?" I asked. "Your husband isn't by the pool. The coast is clear."

"He's on the beach with that yoga floozy," said Beverly. "But they could waltz right by here any minute."

"You can't very well stay in the bushes until they check out," said Nate. "Why don't y'all come on out of there? Let's talk. Maybe there's something we can—"

I gave him a look that said, *What in the name of common sense are you thinking?*

Nate shrugged, gave me a look that said, *What else are we going to do?*

I closed my eyes and gave my head a little shake. It's not that I didn't want to help Beverly and her friend. But we *were* on vacation—with a lot to deal with just then.

On the other hand, Nate was right. What else could we do?

"Beverly, let's go talk about this in your room," I said.

There was more rustling, and then a housekeeping cart rolled out from the other side of the planting bed, followed by two women in housekeeping uniforms. Both ladies sported a headful of beaded baby dreads. I would not've been able to've picked either of them out of a lineup.

Nate and I were momentarily speechless.

Finally, I found my voice. "Y'all did a real good job with the disguises."

"Do you really think so?" asked Beverly.

"How did you come by the housekeeping uniforms?" Nate asked.

"We don't want to get anyone in trouble," said Frankie. "We've been holed up here a few days. We might've made a few new friends sympathetic to our cause."

"And your ... hairdos?" I asked.

Beverly raised a hand to her hair. "Have you seen those open-air taxis? They're like pickup trucks and such, but the backs have bench seats?"

"Sure," I said. These were a popular way of getting around the island.

"Well, we got to talking with Chayla. She drove us to the hotel from the ferry dock the first day we were here? And she took us to the beach ... and a few other places.

She showed us around. Anyway, we admired her hair, and it turns out she does hair as well. Seems like most of the people who live here have to have more than one job. So we called her. It doesn't make for real good sleeping with the beads poking and all, but it does help us blend in."

"Hmm ... well, it definitely is different from your normal hairstyle," I said.

"I'd say it's effective," said Nate. "What exactly were you planning to do dressed like members of the house-keeping staff?"

"Steal a passkey and break into his room, of course," said Frankie. "Now, I can neither confirm nor deny that *stealing* a key would be strictly necessary, so let's say no more about it."

"Okay..." I said. "But what would you have been looking for? If you somehow, mysteriously had a key?"

"I don't know," said Beverly. "Evidence. Listen, we're still nervous being out in the open. The people who really work here know that we don't. And we don't want to get the ones who helped us in trouble on our account. Plus, you never know when Casanova and Jezebel will come in from the beach."

Nate and I stood.

"Let's head back to your room," I said.

We made it back inside without drawing attention to our group, which was a minor miracle. Frankie bolted the door behind us. It was a smallish room with two queen beds with white duvets, imitation wood floors, and light-toned wood built-in furnishings. Floor-length curtains with wide stripes of blue, grey, green, and tan were closed, blocking what was probably a lovely view through the sliding patio doors.

"We made this reservation last minute," said Beverly. "This was the only room they had available. You wouldn't believe what it cost. I made a terrible mistake coming here. I don't know what I was thinking. There's no way to hide the credit card charges." Beverly flopped onto one of the beds. "This is all a nightmare. I just can't believe, after all these years, Melvin would do this to me. I'm the mother of his children. We built a life together. And he's just ... he's trivialized my entire existence." She wiped tears from her cheeks.

Frankie sat beside Beverly and put an arm around her.

Nate and I grabbed the two chairs and leaned into the group sympathetically.

"I know this hurts," I said. "And I know this doesn't help, but sadly, this is a fairly common thing."

"Obviously, the imbecile is having a midlife crisis fling," said Frankie. "And she's right, Beverly. You're not the only one. It's a raging epidemic. Somebody ought to develop a pill for that. Why couldn't he have bought a tiny little convertible with a huge engine like every other respectable man of a certain age?"

"It's perfectly humiliating," said Beverly. "You wouldn't believe the way he's publicly fondling that Romper Room siren. The entire time we've been married, he rarely even so much as held my hand in public. And he's all over her like ... like an *octopus*. What they're doing out on the beach is probably illegal in at least a dozen states. I don't understand. It's like he's a completely different person with her. What's wrong with *me*? Why would he never show me a little affection?"

"Bless your heart." I shook my head. "There's not a single thing wrong with you."

"I told you, Beverly, she's clearly drugged him," said Frankie. "Probably slips a roofie and a Viagra in his coffee every morning."

Just then I was thinking how Frankie seemed a bit preoccupied with other people's pills, either needing them or abusing them.

"I'm just so blasted angry," said Beverly. "Angrier than I've ever been my entire life. All this rage feels like it's just going to erupt out of me any minute now. I'm worried I can't hold it in. I don't know what I might do."

"Maybe some tantrum yoga would help," said Frankie.

They looked at each other and both burst out laughing. They held on to each other and laughed and laughed until they were wiping tears from their eyes.

We laughed along with them, then waited while they composed themselves. "Have y'all had trouble using your cell phones from the hotel?" I asked.

"Yes," said Beverly. "We can't get a signal unless we walk further up the hill."

"Mamma's been trying to get a hold of you," I said. "She was worried."

"We're fine," said Beverly. "Did she … mention anything else?"

"You mean did she get the pictures last night?" I raised an eyebrow at her.

Beverly blushed.

Frankie said, "She was so sweet to offer to help. We don't have any experience with this sort of thing. It was a godsend, us running into her."

What on earth had Mamma led them to believe? That she was an investigator? "She did get pictures, actually. She took quite a few photos of a couple with a substantial age difference having dinner. I understand it was your husband and his mistress. Having dinner, that's not proof of adultery, you understand. But it does look pretty bad, them being here together, especially so close to Christmas."

"Window treatment conference my Aunt Fanny," said Frankie.

"What would we need to prove adultery?" asked Beverly.

"Photos of them in a more compromising position are ideal," said Nate.

"Sadly, those should be easy enough to come by," said Beverly. "Oh dear—how compromising? I mean, I don't think I could possibly—"

I said, "It's also helpful to have hotel receipts. Photos

of them entering and exiting the room together are helpful—in the room together are better still. You typically need a camera with a long-range lens to get the kind of shots you'll need. There are a few other ways to prove they were occupying the same room."

"And then of course," said Nate, "it's best to have an investigator who's documented everything and is able to testify in court. Your testimony wouldn't be as ... unbiased."

"I never dreamed I'd be in this position," said Beverly. "I didn't know what to do. I would've been better off using the money to hire someone than coming down here myself, I guess."

Nate winced, looked at me. I knew exactly what he was thinking. It wouldn't take much time to get the evidence Beverly needed. And we were here. They needed our help. Reluctantly, I nodded at him.

"It seems you ran into the right folks on the beach," said Nate. "How about we make a deal?"

"What sort of deal?" asked Beverly.

"Liz and I will get you the proof you need, and you ladies retire from the detective business ... as does Carolyn."

"How much would that cost?" asked Frankie.

"Consider it a Christmas special," said Nate. "You can hire us for ten dollars."

Beverly looked confused. "Ten dollars an hour isn't very much."

"No, I mean ten dollars in total," said Nate. "Just enough to establish a client relationship."

"I don't understand," said Beverly.

"Mamma is your friend," I said. "You clearly need the help of experienced investigators. We happen to be investigators very experienced in domestic misbehavior, and we're in a position to help. So, let us help you."

"Oh, I couldn't possibly—"

"Consider it a Christmas gift," said Nate, "given in the spirit of the season."

I moved to end debate. "What room number is your husband in?"

"One thousand eleven," said Beverly. "It's in the beachfront building on the far side of the pool."

"All right," said Nate. "You ladies are officially off duty. Relax. Enjoy St. John."

"It's hard to do that," said Frankie. "We lucked up finding out some of their plans because he made reservations in advance, and they were in his emails. But for the most part, we don't know where they're headed, so it's hard to be sure we won't run into them."

"Even with our hair in dreadlocks, it's nerve-wracking," said Beverly. "We keep looking over our shoulder."

"When are they leaving?" asked Nate.

"Saturday—the day after Christmas," said Beverly. "So are we."

"They went to Jolly Mon Grill last night," I said. "They won't be going back there. I mean, it's delicious, but typically folks eat at different restaurants while they're on vacation, right? You could eat there this evening. I highly recommend the paella."

"That's a great idea," said Beverly. "You know, I could turn this into a business trip. Review a few restaurants..."

Nate said, "There you go. And try to relax. What's the worst thing that could happen if you run into them and Melvin recognizes you? He's the one who's cheating. You don't have anything to be ashamed of. Stop hiding in your hotel room so much."

"You make an excellent point," said Beverly.

"If you'd like to have Christmas dinner with us, you're more than welcome," I said. "Someone is making everything ahead of time for us to reheat at our house. I'm sure there'll be plenty. I doubt you'll find restaurants here open Christmas Day. I think folks here tend to celebrate Christmas with family."

"Oh, thank you so much, but we've already imposed on you too much already," said Beverly.

"That's nonsense," I said. "You're not imposing. I invited you. I'm sure Mamma would love to see you. In fact, she'd have my head on a solid silver platter if I allowed you to spend Christmas in a hotel room."

"That's awfully kind of you." Beverly glanced at Frankie for confirmation.

Frankie lifted a shoulder. "If you're sure it's not an intrusion."

"We'll send a car for you," said Nate. "You remember Bartholomew, don't you?"

"The very large, capable man from the beach?" said Beverly. "Of course we remember him. Say, could he help us out with something else while he's here?"

Nate tilted his head, gave a little shrug. "I'm sure he wouldn't mind. What do you need?"

Beverly said, "We need him to dress Melvin in his birthday suit, tie him to one of those wild donkeys, drag him up to the very top of Bordeaux Mountain, then roll him *a-l-l* the way down to the sea to a family of hungry sharks for their supper."

Chapter Six

Usually, Mamma makes chicken and dumplings, Pernil—
a marinated and roasted pork shoulder—and a whole slew
of side dishes for Christmas Eve dinner. Because she knew
we would be in the islands on Christmas Eve, she'd made
that meal for us the Sunday before we left.

That evening, we had our Christmas Eve dinner early.
Something about being in the islands resets my body
clock. I go to bed early, rise with the sun, and my meals
realign accordingly. Everyone else seemed to be on island
time as well. We gathered at four for Christmas cocktails.
Jenny had left a pitcher of something made with pomegranate, cranberry, and tangerines, which was delicious.
Christmas music played throughout the house.

Nate grilled steaks for us on the oversized grill on the
deck at Cinnamon Ridge. He and I plated the filets atop
buttery grilled slices of French bread, then crowned the

steaks with crab cakes, and finished the dish with a generous ladle of Hollandaise sauce and a sprinkle of green onions. We served the steaks with mashed potatoes, roasted asparagus, and additional French bread.

By five p.m., everyone was seated at the large outdoor table overlooking the Atlantic and the British Virgin Islands beyond. Everyone held hands and Mamma spoke for the group, as is her custom, thanking God for our many blessings. Then, Nate and I ferried the plates out and set them at each place. The oohing and aching commenced.

"Now that's impressive." Bartholomew's voice was nearly reverent.

Blake made an appreciative half grunt, half growl noise as he tasted his first bite.

"Son," admonished Mamma. Then she turned to Nate. "My goodness, this looks like something straight out of a fancy restaurant. You are such a good cook, Nate."

"Carolyn, all I did was grill the steaks. Your daughter did the hard parts."

"Steak's the best part," said Blake. "This is perfect. You can't get steaks grilled this good in restaurants. Man." He delivered another bite to his mouth. His eyes rolled back in his head. You won't find many people who appreciate a good steak as much as my brother.

For a few minutes, the only sounds were cutlery on plates and the sweet tone of Joan Osborne's voice singing "Angels We Have Heard on High." Nate and I had this meal in a restaurant once years ago and loved it so much we'd recreated it at home. It was our favorite celebratory meal for a reason.

"Liz, this is amazing," said Poppy. "Just delicious." With a grin and a gleam in her eye, she looked from me to Blake, then back. "You'll have to help me learn how to do this. I think this recipe might come in handy."

"You learn how to make this, I'll do anything you ask," said Blake.

"I would imagine you would do anything for the mother of your child regardless." Mamma gave him The Look.

Blake tilted his head from side to side and gestured with his free hand. "Of course, Mom. But, man ... this is just fabulous. That's all I'm saying."

Joe scrutinized Merry. "And you're sure you don't cook at all? It seems unlikely. Your mother is the Southern Julia Child. Your sister obviously inherited her skill. Maybe we should get you some pots and pans and just see what happens."

Blake barked out a laugh. "Best case scenario, she'd burn down the house."

Daddy said, "Don't hold your breath on that one, son."

"I can cook you a bowl of cereal anytime you like," said Merry.

I rolled my eyes, looked at Joe. "She could cook if she wanted to."

Merry shook her head. "It's just not my gift." That was her story, and she would stick to it like someone had affixed it with Gorilla Glue.

"No one will want my plain country cooking after eating all this fancy food," said Mamma.

Merry and I exchanged a glance, then turned to Mamma.

"I can't imagine in what universe your spreads would be considered 'plain country cooking,'" said Merry.

"Mamma, this is a very simple meal compared to your Christmas Eve dinners," I said.

"Well," said Mamma, "I don't make anything this fancy. Just basic meat and vegetables."

I suppressed an eye roll, but had to chuckle. Mamma was a legendary cook, and there was nothing basic about anything she'd ever made.

Focused on his dinner, Daddy was uncharacteristically quiet.

"I thought Jenny was doing the cooking," said Mamma.

"She's doing most of it," I said. "But Nate and I like to cook. We didn't want to do it every night, but we thought we'd mix it up."

For the next few minutes, we admired the view and enjoyed our dinner. A warm, gentle breeze wafted by. "Silent Night" played softly through the sound system. It was a perfect evening—all surely was calm and bright.

"If it's all right with everyone, we thought we'd spend

tomorrow here," said Nate. "Not much on the island is open Christmas Day. We're well provisioned, so we can just relax. I know that's kind of a repeat of today for most of us... I'd hate for anyone to be bored."

Nate so wanted everything to be perfect. And his original plan had us on a sailboat all day Christmas Eve, which would've made tomorrow a welcome break.

"Darlin', I've told you," said Mamma. "This place is just Heaven on earth. I could happily spend every day of our trip right here. What more could we want?"

Everyone else echoed her thoughts.

"There're some puzzles and games on the bookcase in our room," said Merry. "At least one of the puzzles is Christmas themed. I'll bring it up after dinner."

"Oh, I'd love a Christmas puzzle," said Mamma.

"What happened to those Christmas cookies?" asked Daddy. "Those looked mighty good."

"I don't know where they got to," I said innocently. "But we have salted caramel cheesecake for dessert."

"Now that sounds mighty fine." Bartholomew spoke up.

Just then I was thinking how, like the rest of the men I knew, the way to Bart's heart was definitely through his stomach. I was highly interested in keeping him happy, so this was good information.

"Didn't you take those cookies to someone?" asked Blake. "I thought y'all took them with you when you went out this morning."

I should've known Blake would be on top of any food-related developments.

"Oh—I'd forgotten." I smiled brightly. "You're right. Yes, we did."

Blake looked at me expectantly, waiting for me to elaborate on the fate of the Christmas cookies.

"Who wants cheesecake?" I asked.

"Where'd you take the cookies?" Daddy's face wrinkled in confusion. Mamma failed to call him out on that.

I tilted my head at him. "I thought you loved cheesecake."

"Course I do," said Daddy. "But it's Christmas time. We always have Christmas cookies. Those thumbprint ones are my favorite. I saw some of those in that basket."

"Do y'all have friends here?" asked Blake.

"We do, as a matter of fact," said Nate. "But we gave the cookies to the ladies we met on the beach yesterday —the ones from the Upstate? They're here by themselves over the holidays. It just seemed like a nice gesture."

Daddy nodded, but he looked vaguely disgruntled. "What are they doing down here by themselves at Christmastime? Don't they have families? Where are their husbands?"

I sensed the serenity of the evening slipping away.

Mamma arched an eyebrow at Daddy. "Indeed. They do. Well, Beverly does. I'm not sure about Frankie. She didn't mention it."

"Well, where's the woman's husband at?" Daddy asked.

"The ladies in question have names, Franklin," said Mamma. "Beverly and Frankie. And not that it's any of your business whatsoever, but Beverly does, in fact, have a husband—a sorry one at that. He's at the Westin, as we speak, with a girl who either suffers from loose morals, or is horribly misguided, or who is possibly being held against her will. The only thing one can say for absolute certain is that she's young enough to be his granddaughter." Mamma fixed Daddy with a Look. "Is there anything else you'd like to know, Franklin?"

"As a matter of fact, there is." Daddy's dander was up as well. "I'd like to know if that was her sorry husband you were taking pictures of last night in the restaurant."

"And what if it was?" asked Mamma.

"Why would you do such a thing?" asked Daddy. "What do you think you are, a detective?"

"I think I'm a woman who wanted to help another woman in a bind," said Mamma.

"Seriously, Mom?" said Blake. "That kind of thing can lead to all kinds of trouble. What if you get called to testify in court? That man might not take kindly to your interfering in his business. We don't know anything about him —about any of them, really."

"That could've been dangerous," said Merry. "But how exciting! Mamma goes undercover."

Daddy was agitated. He gave Merry a look that said,

Hush, child. "It absolutely was dangerous ... and ... unseemly."

"*Unseemly?*" Mamma's voice rose three octaves. "*You,* Frank, are lecturing *me* on unseemly behavior?"

Warning lights, bells, and whistles went off in my head, likely my sister's too.

"Is anyone thirsty?" I asked. "I'm thirsty. Why don't I open some more wine? Who wants red?"

"I'd love some," said Merry. "Red wine will be good with the cheesecake. Mamma, what do you think with the cheesecake, a red blend, or a merlot?"

Mamma was having none of being distracted. "For Heaven's sake ... I was in a crowded restaurant, surrounded by all of you. There wasn't a thing unseemly about my behavior. And I am highly offended by the very suggestion. And as far as being dangerous is concerned, it's not like I was being shot at in an alley, or any one of the numerous other places our daughter has been on the business end of a firearm."

"That's a whole nother problem. And a serious one," said Daddy. "But I cannot believe you would—"

"Pardon me, Frank ... y'all everything is completely under control," said Nate. "Liz and I have spoken with the ladies in question, and they've agreed—as has Carolyn—to discontinue their investigative endeavors. Those folks are leaving the island on Saturday, and everything's all settled."

"But you're not—" Daddy started.

"Not what, Frank? Smart enough to take pictures?" Mamma's tone was testy.

"Smart's got nothing to do with it," said Daddy.

"So you bribed those women with the cookies?" asked Blake.

"You know," said Nate, "I believe those cookies actually came from a bakery. I bet you anything we can get another basket of them. Two, if you like. Enough to last us a few days."

"Now that's a fine idea," said Daddy.

"And trust us, this situation with the women from the Upstate is completely under control," I said. "Let's all just enjoy some dessert, shall we?"

"Oh dear." Mamma swallowed hard. "Nate, please forgive my grievous lapse in manners. I'm afraid I lost my mind there for a moment." She glared at Daddy.

"Nonsense, Carolyn," said Nate. "We're just having a spirited discussion here. That's one of the things I love best about this family. We're all so wonderfully open with each other. None of us ever has to worry about ulterior motives, hidden agendas, or false pretenses."

"What kind of cheesecake did you say it was?" Bartholomew smiled, but raised his voice slightly, in what I took to be an effort to help steer the conversation in a new direction. Bart was the only one at the table other than me who knew Nate's secret.

Nate flushed like maybe he just realized what he'd said,

and it had hit him how he wasn't being very open. His eyes found mine. What were we going to do?

I hopped up. "It's salted caramel cheesecake, and I'm getting us all a slice right now."

Later, after we'd had dessert and collaborated on kitchen cleanup, Nate and I sat alone in lounge chairs by the pool looking up at the countless glittering stars scattered across the black velvet sky.

"It's amazing, isn't it?" asked Nate. "There are so many stars in the Stella Maris night sky, but you can see even more of them here. There's less light pollution, less stuff in the air..."

"It's positively magical."

"When you look at that, it's not quite so hard to wrap your brain around the idea that there are more stars in the known universe than grains of sand on the earth."

"I still can't wrap my brain around Mamma embarking on an investigation," I said.

"And I can't stop thinking about what she said," said Nate. "The part about how many times you've been shot at."

"Sweetheart, seriously," I said. "She was deflecting."

"Maybe so," said Nate. "But she wasn't wrong."

"And I'm sitting right here beside you, completely fine."

"By the grace of God," said Nate, "And Colleen's regular intervention, which I suppose is the same thing ... and possibly Bart's intervention as well. What I'm saying here, is you've been lucky. And I don't want that luck to run out."

"You're the one who had a gunshot wound. And you're the one who nearly died tackling a killer in a running leap off our deck," I said.

He nodded. "And then there was the incident on I-26 with the Explorer. And the incident with the *other* Explorer on the ferry. And the Explorer that exploded. What I'm saying here is, we have very dangerous jobs. Your mamma isn't wrong about that."

"It's in the job description," I said. "We've both known that from the beginning. We made that choice, both of us."

"You're right, we did. But Slugger, it doesn't have to be a forever thing. We could make new choices."

I turned to him. "Do you really want to do that? I thought you loved what we do."

"I do," he said. "But I love you more. And I think it's best we tell everyone about the money. It's true that money can be a mixed blessing. Sometimes it messes things up, but secrets are so much worse. It was the hardest thing I've ever done, keeping all that from you."

"If you're sure that's what you want to do," I said. "It's your secret ... just pick the time you think is right and tell them."

"Maybe I should do it and get it over with," he said. "That should put a stop to anyone else trying to pay for dinner while we're here, anyway. As it is, things are a bit awkward."

We went back to watching the stars.

"Back to possibly making new choices ... there's something else to consider here," he said. "Have you ever thought about how similar St. John is to Stella Maris in some ways?"

"Sure," I said. "The similarities are obvious. They're both pristine islands, both accessible only by boat..."

"And they both face challenges with development, controlling it ... and with evacuating for storms."

The recurring nightmare I'd had for years popped into my head. "I see what you're saying, but what does that have to do with our jobs?"

"What if we had new jobs?" he asked.

"What kind of jobs?" I felt my face scrunch.

"Less dangerous ones, for starters, but jobs that dealt more directly with protecting Stella Maris. I've been thinking about this a lot ... just hear me out."

"I'm listening."

"What if we started a foundation with the mission of protecting Stella Maris? We could make that our focus ... study better home design, better erosion control. We could maybe donate some land to the park service, the way Laurence Rockefeller did when the national park was created here on St. John. And that's just to get started. We could educate ourselves better on ways to make it safer for everyone who lives on Stella Maris."

"I don't know what to say," I said. "Everything has happened so fast. I mean, of course we have options I never dreamed of. But I have to tell you, I love our life exactly as it is."

"And so do I," said Nate. "But that doesn't mean I wouldn't love it just as much if we had different—safer—jobs. I love *you*. And I want to keep you safe. And frankly, I want to live to grow old with you and sit in rocking chairs on the front porch and watch Blake and Poppy's grandkids play in the yard."

"I want that too," I said. "That's a lot to think about."

"Well, just think about it. We don't have to decide right now."

"I will."

And then my phone rang. Mamma's face was on the screen.

"Mamma? Why are you—"

"We've got to get over to the Westin," she said.

"What's wrong?"

"Beverly and Frankie called. They had to climb to the top of a hill to call me. They didn't have your number." Mamma's voice quivered.

"Mamma? What's wrong?"

"Melvin's dead."

Chapter Seven

Frankie opened the door to their room before we could knock. We rushed inside. She stuck her nose out the door, looked both ways down the hall, then closed the door behind us. Beverly was huddled on the bed farthest from the door, arms wrapped around herself, rocking back and forth. She shivered uncontrollably, like her bones were made of ice.

"What's happened?" I asked.

"Mel-vin is d-ead." Beverly's teeth chattered.

After peeking out the patio door curtains as if the devil himself might be out there, Frankie sat by Beverly and wrapped the blanket tighter around her shoulders.

Nate and I pulled up the chairs we'd occupied earlier. All I could think about was the two men following Melvin and his girlfriend after we'd left Jolly Mon Grill. Was there more to that than we'd thought?

"How?" asked Nate.

"We don't know what happened to him," said Frankie.

"Where is he?" I asked.

"In his room," said Beverly.

"And the two of you were there because..." I waited for them to fill in the blanks.

Beverly winced. "Remember when y'all said we shouldn't hide anymore?"

"Well, yes," I said. "We did encourage you to relax and enjoy St. John ... not fret so much about running into Melvin and his mistress."

"We might've taken that a tiny bit further than y'all intended," said Frankie.

"In what way, exactly?" asked Nate.

"We had an early dinner. And we had a couple of these Christmas special cocktails..." Beverly glanced at Frankie.

"Mistletoe Margaritas," said Frankie. "Tequila and cranberry juice, triple sec, and lime."

Beverly nodded. "We had a couple of those. Each. I might've had three. Neither of us are typically big drinkers, but ... well, the situation called for liquor on several levels. And then I started feeling all brave, like I wanted to confront Melvin. You were right, I decided. *I* had nothing to be ashamed of. *He* was the one who betrayed our wedding vows. I wanted to give him a piece of my mind ... and maybe a swift kick. But I swear, I didn't touch him."

"So you went to his room?" I prompted.

Beverly nodded, but then went to dry sobbing and couldn't get the words out.

"We let ourselves in with the key we'd gotten with our housekeeping outfits," said Frankie. "We were hoping to catch them in the act, so to speak. Beverly could give him a piece of her mind, and we could get that evidence of adultery ourselves and save y'all the trouble. We just hated infringing on your family vacation."

"What happened next?" asked Nate.

"Nothing—I swear," Beverly stammered, then took a deep breath and let it out slowly, seemed to gather herself. "He was lying in the floor by the bed, just sprawled there. It was obvious something was bad wrong. We tried to wake him up, thinking maybe he'd gotten drunk and passed out. When he wouldn't respond at all, I checked for a pulse. But there wasn't one." The last part came out as a wail.

"We just panicked and bolted from the room," said Frankie. "We ran up the hill to where we could get a cell signal and called Carolyn. That was the only way we knew to get ahold of y'all."

"You didn't report this to anyone?" I asked.

"No," said Beverly. "We were petrified it looked like we'd killed him. Listen, I'm highly claustrophobic. I couldn't possibly survive going to jail."

"What about his girlfriend?" asked Nate.

"*She* is nowhere to be found," said Beverly. "She must've killed him, right?"

"He was fully clothed," said Frankie. "It wasn't a clear case of death by nookie."

"It's impossible to know what happened with the information we have right now," I said. "Did he have any health problems? A heart condition, maybe?"

"No," said Beverly, "not that we were aware of, anyway. He had regular physicals and all."

"Let's arrange for the hotel staff to find him," said Nate, "and then let the local authorities handle it. It's more likely than not he died of natural causes. The girl-friend probably got scared and ran off."

"But won't they suspect us?" asked Beverly.

"Not if he died of a heart attack," I said. "Let's not panic and assume the worst-case scenario. It's highly unlikely he's been murdered."

Frankie tucked the blanket around Beverly's shoulders tighter and rubbed her back. "You see? It's going to be fine. No need to panic."

"But Melvin's dead." Beverly's expression was grief-stricken. "We'll never patch things up. The last thing he said to me was a lie. After all those years together, I just can't belief this is how our story ends."

Frankie drew a long breath and let it out slowly. "Honey, let's call Delta and see about getting you home right away. You can grieve there."

"I can't leave him here," she said. "There will be

arrangements to be made. I have to get *him* home, so we can give him a proper funeral. I have to tell our children."

"Of course," I said. "The first step is to turn this over to the local authorities so we can start the process. And the cleanest way to do that is for the hotel staff to discover the body."

"We need for someone in that room to request something from housekeeping, or the front desk," said Nate. "Something they'd leave in the room if no one answered the door."

"There's going to be a record in the system of Beverly and Frankie entering the room—well, of housekeeping using a key card to enter the room," I said.

"Nothing to be done about that now," said Nate. "Besides, if he died of natural causes, it won't matter. No one will be checking the records."

"We need to order some towels," I said. "But we need to do it from Melvin's room. Can we have that key card?"

Frankie crossed the room, got it from her purse, and handed it to me.

"You ladies wait here," said Nate. "We'll be back shortly."

Nate and I headed out towards Melvin's room.

"Let's try the patio door first," I said as we crossed the property. "That building has oceanfront rooms. Maybe he was on the patio and came in for a drink or something. He might've been planning to go back out. If we're lucky, he didn't lock the door."

"I had the exact same thought," said Nate.

We rounded the building. Based on the room number, Melvin's room was second from the end. Fortunately, no one else in that building was on their veranda just then. We stepped onto the small patio. I turned my back to the door to watch for passersby. Everything seemed quiet. Night had fallen hard over the island. It was pitch black already, and only seven p.m.

Close to shore, a boat engine roared to life. Our heads swiveled, eyes scanning the water, but it was too dark to see. The motor seemed to have a misfire, making a chug-chug-gasp-chug noise. The racket faded as the boat motored out of the bay.

Nate tried the door.

"We're in." He slid the door open and we both stepped inside.

Melvin's room was larger than Beverly and Frankie's. There was a separate sitting area, with a bedroom to the side. Nate and I swept both rooms with our eyes, then did it again. Then we checked the bathroom.

The suite was empty.

No Melvin, dead or alive.

"I guess he wasn't dead after all," I said.

Nate knelt by the bed. "Wherever he went, he went without these." He held a pair of wire-rimmed glasses. The frame was slightly twisted, and one of the lenses was smashed. "These are bifocals."

"That's not a good sign at all." I stepped over to the wardrobe. "His clothes are here, but no sign of hers."

Next, I went back into the bathroom. Upon closer inspection, it was devoid of the typical female lotions and potions. "Well, for sure she's cleared out," I said.

We proceeded back into the living area.

"I have a feeling Melvin has met with some misfortune more sinister than a heart attack," said Nate.

Colleen appeared in a spray of golden, glittery light. "Time to go. Fast."

Nate and I darted towards the patio door.

Just then, someone knocked three times on the door to the hallway. "Housekeeping."

I slid the door closed and we bolted towards the beach. From a safe distance, we watched as a team of maids began cleaning the room. As quickly as she'd popped in, Colleen popped back out.

"Housekeeping doesn't generally clean this time of night, on Christmas Eve at that." I said. "This is very odd."

"The only reason they'd do that would be they had a checkout and needed to turn the room," said Nate.

"I'm led to wonder if perhaps the room's last occupant didn't leave by boat," I said.

We both stared out into the bay.

"I wouldn't bet against that," said Nate.

"It's odd, Colleen showing up, isn't it?" I mused. "This

is definitely outside her mission. Beverly, Frankie, Melvin ... these folks don't have anything to do with Stella Maris. And Colleen's definitely minding the rules right now."

"It's unexpected, sure enough," said Nate.

We walked back to Beverly and Frankie's room. Frankie let us in and closed the door quickly behind us. "What do you think? He *is* dead, right?"

"We can't say for certain," I said. "But if he is, someone's moved his body."

"*What?*" Both women spoke at the same time.

Nate added. "While there're no obvious sign of violence, it would appear he most likely met with foul play."

"I knew it," said Beverly. "That limber Lolita killed him."

"That's possible," I said, "but we don't know that yet. And frankly, I seriously doubt she could've moved his body by herself."

"Why would she have done that?" asked Beverly. "Where would she take him?"

"We ran off in such a hurry, we didn't even get a good look around," said Frankie. "Did y'all see any blood? We didn't see any blood..."

"No." Nate shook his head. "Nothing like that. Nothing was disturbed."

Frankie tilted her head and looked confused. "I thought you said he met with foul play."

"We found his glasses," I said. "They'd been pushed up under the bed. They were broken."

"He can't see a thing without them," said Beverly. "I tried to get him to have the laser surgery. He'd never go off without his glasses."

"Did you find a weapon?" asked Frankie. "Maybe a broken lamp? Or do you think he was poisoned? Was there a glass of anything on the nightstand? Maybe the suspicious smell of bitter almonds? I *wish* we'd paid more attention while we were in that room."

I cast her a sideways glance. Was Frankie perhaps a crime drama fan?

"Nothing like that at all," Nate reiterated. "But that doesn't mean—"

"We need Horatio Caine's crew," Frankie interrupted.

"I'm sorry—*who*?" I asked.

"From CSI," Frankie said, as if our credentials were in serious question because we hadn't known. "Miami," she added, like that should clear things up.

"Hmmm," mused Nate. "I'm afraid at this point, a good forensics team might find evidence the two of you were in the room this evening."

Both women inhaled sharply.

"What now?" asked Frankie.

Nate stepped over to the room phone and checked the information on the side, then tapped the number into his iPhone. "Yes, could I have Melvin Baker's room, please? ...

I'm sorry? ... Has he checked out then? ... What about a..."
he looked at us blankly.

"What's the yoga instructor's name?" I asked.

"Starla," said Beverly. "Starla Douglas."

"How about a Starla Douglas?" Nate said into the
phone. "Ah ... right. Thank you for checking."

He ended the call and handed the phone to me.
"There's no one registered here by either of those names.
No one in the system who might've recently checked out.
No Melvin at all, and no Starla."

"But that's impossible," said Beverly.

"Maybe they checked in under aliases," said Frankie.
"Or someone with the hotel is in on it. Could be a
conspiracy."

"Could it just be someone at the front desk made a
simple mistake?" asked Beverly.

"If Melvin or Starla either one were available for
comment, I'd say sure," I said. "But since they've both
gone missing, I'm inclined to think not. Somehow, they've
been wiped from the system."

"That points to someone else being involved," said
Nate. "Could be an employee was paid to remove them
from the hotel's records. There are several possibilities."

"I'm scared," said Beverly. "This is ... something is very
wrong here. Won't they know you're the one who called?
Surely, they have caller ID."

"I put in a code to hide my number," said Nate.

"What do we do?" Frankie had taken to pacing.

Wringing her hands, she turned to me, a plea in her eyes. "What now?"

"Your tickets home are for Saturday?" asked Nate.

"Yes," said Beverly.

"Let's get you ladies packed," said Nate. "You've had a change in itinerary."

"I beg your pardon?" said Beverly.

Nate looked at me. "Let's chat outside, shall we? Would you ladies excuse us for a moment?"

I nodded. "Y'all go ahead and pack. We'll all sleep better tonight if y'all sleep somewhere else."

Nate and I walked out onto the patio.

"Where do you want to take them?" I asked.

"I don't know what Melvin got himself involved in," said Nate, "but my guess is it's gotten him killed."

"I can't think Beverly and Frankie are involved in whatever happened to him," I said.

"Of course not," said Nate. "But there's too much we don't know here. Whoever killed Melvin could be watching Beverly, for all we know. If the killer moved his body in that boat we heard earlier, it's possible they saw us going into his room. It's worrisome.

"It's dark out," he continued, "but there's more light onshore around the resort where we were than on the water. Remember the conversation we were having earlier? Your safety is my first priority. I want to keep these ladies safe, but I also don't want to draw trouble to our door. Maybe we should get them a room at another hotel."

"On Christmas Eve?" I asked. "That might prove difficult."

"It's doable, I think. It's early yet. I know some of the local innkeepers." He massaged his neck. "On the other hand, let's just fly them home. I sent the plane back to get Bart some help. They should've landed by now. We don't need it for another ten days."

Nate's phone rang. "Bart. Everything okay?"

Nate's eyes locked on mine, an expression in them I'd seldom seen.

Panic.

He took a deep breath, swallowed. "All right. You stay there and hold down the fort. We'll be back as soon as we can." He ended the call, ran a hand over his face.

"Poppy's missing," he said.

"*What?*"

"She went to lie down. Blake just went to check on her, and she's not there."

"Is—"

He shook his head. "Everyone else is fine."

"But—"

"No one heard a thing. They were all upstairs. You know how thick those walls are. Blake and Poppy's room is right by the stairs to the driveway."

"Maybe she went for a walk? Maybe she—"

"There's a note."

Something hard rammed me in the stomach, leaving me breathless.

Nate said, "Someone wants us to leave the island now —we have two hours—fly home, forget we ever heard the name Melvin Baker. No police. We agree not to investigate at all. And wire a million dollars to an offshore account. If we do all of those things, we're assured Poppy will be delivered to the Charleston airport unharmed by four p.m. on Monday."

"Oh please, God, no." I gasped for breath. This couldn't be happening.

He grabbed my shoulders. "Liz, look at me."

I met his eyes. The panic had been replaced with steel.

"We will fix this. Poppy will be fine. Right now— whoever has her—she is their only leverage with us. They will not hurt her."

He was right. I prayed he was right. "But ... who? What is the connection between Melvin Baker and Poppy?"

"I'm afraid we are."

Of course. That had to be it. Whoever killed Melvin knew we were here, were involved. They'd likely seen us going into Melvin's room. And they'd made a call. But to who? Maybe someone was watching our house after last night. They had to've been nearby, at any rate. They'd gone straight to the house and grabbed Poppy as leverage —to keep us from calling the police or getting any more involved. And somehow, they knew we could pay a million-dollar ransom.

Nate slid a look around the grounds. "Let's get back

inside." He pulled the door open, waited for me to walk through it, then followed.

"Ladies, there's been a disturbing development," said Nate. "I think it's best if we get y'all safely home as soon as possible. As it turns out, we're going to be heading back to South Carolina tonight. Our plane is at the airport in St. Thomas. The crew will take you to Ohio after they drop us off in Charleston. Which airport did you fly out of? Cleveland?"

I stared at Nate. Surely, he didn't seriously plan on us leaving without Poppy?

Beverly stood, a determined look on her tearstained face. "I appreciate what you're trying to do here. But I can't leave without knowing what's happened to Melvin. I owe that to our children."

"Beverly, I understand how you must feel," I said. "But the most important thing here is to get you safely home to your children. They've apparently lost one parent already."

"I'm sorry," she said. "I just can't. I need to know what happened to him."

"But you and Frankie are not equipped to investigate this," I said gently. "And ... things have escalated."

"What do you mean?" Beverly looked bewildered.

"Escalated from murder?" Frankie put a fine point on the matter. "Are we dealing with a serial killer situation?"

"If we just *leave*, there won't be an investigation at all," said Beverly. "What do you mean, 'escalated'?"

"And if you stay," I said, "and report Melvin missing —if they even take that report in the circumstances—you run the risk of becoming suspects yourselves. I'm recalling that you suffer from claustrophobia?"

"I'll have to take that risk." The note of stubborn in Beverly's voice reminded me of Mamma.

"Beverly, please be reasonable," said Nate. "We just want to get you out of harm's way."

"I know," she said, "and I really do appreciate that. Frankie and I both appreciate everything you've done."

"I have an idea," said Frankie.

We all turned towards her.

To Beverly, she said, "What if we hired Liz and Nate to look into this? I don't mean like before, when they were going to get pictures of Melvin for ten dollars. I mean, really hire them? To find out what happened to Melvin? It's not like you have to explain where the money went anymore. Think about it ... we'd have our own investigative team. That'd be much better than trying to deal with the local police. Liz and Nate won't go off on some wild tangent thinking we did this."

"Would y'all be willing to do that?" asked Beverly. "I could go home in peace. Frankie, that's a brilliant idea. Let the professionals handle it."

"Unfortunately—" Nate started, then switched gears. "First, that won't be necessary. As we mentioned, there's been a further development."

"Who has escalated what?" asked Beverly. "What are you not telling us?"

I looked at Nate.

He nodded.

"You remember my sister-in-law, Poppy, from the beach?" I asked. "She's been kidnapped."

"What?" Beverly looked bewildered. "But what does that have to do with—"

"Whoever has taken her wants us to walk away from whatever has happened to your husband," I said. "No police, no investigation."

"That makes no sense." Frankie's entire face puckered into an expression of disbelief.

"We've clearly stumbled into something highly dangerous that we know very little about," said Nate. "But—and here's the most salient point right now—we have very little time to find Poppy. Every moment is critical. The only way we can also ensure *your* safety is if you get on the plane right away. Liz and I have a job to do here. So ... can we offer you a lift back to Ohio?"

"I thought you said you were leaving too," said Beverly.

"Most of our party will be flying out shortly," said Nate. "Would you like to go with them?"

Frankie said, "Beverly, we need to go. We aren't equipped for this, and we're slowing these nice folks down. We can't have that on us—that something bad happened to Poppy because we got in the way. Let's go home. We'll figure out what to do about Melvin from there. Maybe talk to a lawyer. Didn't Linda Parker's son go to law school? I think he handled our neighbor's real estate closing."

"Good idea," said Nate. "Now, you ladies wait here. Someone from my team will come to the door and give you the password 'mistletoe.' Don't open the door for anyone else. He will get you safely to the plane. As soon as you land, call an attorney. A criminal attorney. One who's been out of law school a while."

Chapter Eight

Bart stood by the sliding door in the dining area at Cinnamon Ridge, rage radiating off him in waves. "I failed to do my job."

"You can't be everywhere at once," said Nate. "I should've authorized backup, had the rest of your team here sooner. This is not your fault. And we don't have time to play the blame game."

"Someone's on the way to pick up the ladies at the Westin," said Bart. "Everyone else is beating the bushes, looking for leads."

Nate nodded and took a seat at one end of the dining table. Blake sat at the other end, and the rest of us were gathered around it. My brother appeared to have aged a decade since dinner. "This makes no sense whatsoever," he said. "Where would I—a small town police chief—get a million dollars?"

Nate put his elbows on the table and leaned in. "I need to tell you all something. I'll explain things more fully when we have more time. The short version is my grandfather left me quite a lot of money. I had to keep that from Liz until our first anniversary, which, as you know, was Sunday. Whoever took Poppy knows that I can pay the ransom. And of course, I *will* pay the ransom. We will do whatever we need to do to ensure Poppy's safety. All of our safety."

Everyone except Bart stared at Nate, shell-shocked looks on their faces.

"Now," said Nate, "Liz and I came up with a plan on our way back to the house. We're thinking we have to look like we're doing what they asked. We need to get to the airport and get on the plane as soon as possible. Four more members of my security team landed not long ago. They will meet us at the airport. We have to assume someone is watching to see us get on the plane and take off. Liz, Bart, and I will change clothes with three of them, and they will get on board in our place. We will circle back to St. John and find Poppy. The plane will take you all home, drop Beverly and Frankie in Ohio, then turn around and come back for us."

"I am not leaving this island without Poppy." Blake enunciated each word clearly, his voice ragged but firm.

Nate nodded. "I figured as much. We'll put the fourth member of the team on the plane in your place. Frank, Joe, that leaves the two of you to escort Carolyn,

Merry, and the ladies from Ohio home. Y'all all right with that?"

"Whatever you need," said Joe.

"I'll stay here," said Daddy. "You need all the help you can get."

Nate shook his head. "I appreciate that. But we don't have another person to put on the plane in your place. We can't risk whoever has taken Poppy figuring out some of us are still here."

"This is all my fault." Mamma was in tears. She covered her mouth with both hands and shook her head.

"No, Mamma," I said. "You can't think that way. We don't know really, what all is going on here yet. But it certainly is not your fault."

"If only I hadn't—"

"Mamma," I said, "I'm so sorry. But we just can't do this right now. We will get Poppy back safe. But we've got to move."

"Bart?" Nate gave him a look filled with meaning only the two of them understood.

Bart lifted a heavy-duty duffel bag from the floor and set it on the table. "Some things you don't pack for vacation, and you hope to never need. This is the predicament pouch." He unzipped it. Inside, foam compartments held my Sig 9—or one identical to it—Nate's Glock, and six other handguns.

Nate and I retrieved our weapons.

"Bart is already armed," said Nate. "Does anyone not know how to use a firearm?"

"I've never fired one," said Merry. "I don't think I could."

Joe selected a Glock. "That's all right. I have, and I can."

Bart picked up one of the pistols. "This is actually a stun gun. In case of emergency." He handed it to Merry.

She took it from him hesitantly.

"I'll show you how to use it," said Joe.

Everyone else chose a weapon and took a box of ammunition.

"Grab what's essential," said Nate. "Whatever you leave behind, we'll have it shipped later. Everyone in the Jeeps. Let's go."

Chapter Nine

To make it look good, we took all four of the Jeeps. Mamma and Daddy rode with Bart. Blake, Joe, and Nate drove the other three. This arrangement left Nate and me alone in our Jeep. I'd long since given up calling for Colleen when I wanted her, but I was praying she'd join us. She popped in just as we turned onto North Shore Road.

"Don't get on the plane," she said.

"I have two preflight inspection teams covering every square inch of the plane as we speak," said Nate. "I've already thought about sabotage."

"*What?*" My mind whirled. "You're thinking they mean to kill us all?"

"Think about it," said Nate. "That would be the only way to make sure we don't report ... hell, I'm not even sure what we *could* report. We never even saw Melvin Baker's body."

"But his wife and her friend did," said Colleen. "These people are the kind who are very careful to never leave loose ends."

"Who exactly are these people?" I heard the anger and fear in my own voice.

"I can't tell you that," she said. "I'll be with Poppy until you find her. Whatever you do, none of you get on that plane."

Relief flooded through me. Colleen was with Poppy—of course she was. This was well within her jurisdiction. Poppy carried the next generation of people Colleen needed for her mission. The baby was the reason Colleen was here. I wished, not for the first time, I could explain Colleen to the rest of our family. It would give them peace to know we had help more powerful than any of us mere mortals could provide.

"What about a charter flight?" asked Nate.

Colleen was quiet for a moment. She looked Heaven-ward and prayed. Soft white light radiated from her. After a moment, she grabbed Nate's shoulder and said, "Do not even get on a ferry to St. Thomas tonight. No charter flight. No airport at all. Stay here. Transportation is perilous tonight. *No ferries of any kind.*"

"Naturally." Nate shook his head. "I should've seen that one coming. We frequently have bad luck with ferries."

"But what about—" I started.

"I have to go." Colleen whooshed through the top of the Jeep in a stream of silvery light.

Nate pulled the Jeep into the parking lot at Trunk Bay. The other three Jeeps in our convoy pulled in behind us. Everyone hopped out, talking all at once, asking questions we couldn't answer.

"New plan," said Nate. "Give me five minutes. Everyone, please stay as quiet as possible."

He jogged over to the other side of the parking lot, made a few calls, then dashed back. "So listen, we need a place to lay low here on St. John. It's Christmas Eve, and there's not much available. I have a friend who works for the park service, and he's worked us into a few of the cottages at Cinnamon Bay campground. We were lucky to get these. A big group got snowed in somewhere, apparently. Now, I know these accommodations are quite a bit more rustic than what we normally enjoy. But ... actually, I think this will be perfect. It's the last place anyone would think to look. And we won't be quite so isolated there. It's not far—just two bays to the east. Bart, would you call and arrange for Beverly and Frankie to be brought there?"

Bart nodded once. "On it. And rolling." He hopped in his Jeep.

Everyone else followed suit.

Chapter Ten

Cinnamon Bay Campground was arranged with one parking lot close to the road. From there, you walk down a path to the check-in desk and restaurant. Beyond that, paths take you to the various sections of the park: tent campsites, eco-tent camping, cottages, et cetera. Inside the park, you'll also find several archeological sites, one of them circa AD 1, the ruins of an estate house circa AD 1680, a Taino ceremonial site, and an eroding village and cemetery of those enslaved on the former plantation between the 1600s and 1840s. It was an interesting place with a long history, some of it very dark indeed.

We got everyone settled into five of the small, concrete cottages by the beach. They were basic, but clean and quirky, and would've been a lot of fun in better circumstances, in a rustic hippie sort of way. With louvered doors and windows, they each had a small bedroom and separate living space with a table and chairs and dorm-size refrigerator. Cooking was meant to be done on the patio, where there was a grill, additional cooking supplies, a picnic table, and Adirondack chairs. At that moment, we were all in shock. No one was concerned about the accommodations.

"I'm such a wreck," said Mamma. "I'm so turned around I can't find the powder room. Where is it, Sugar?"

"Come on, Mamma, I'll take you." I gentled her out the door.

It was inky black outside. By the light from the flashlight utility on my cell phone, I pulled my bewildered Mamma down a path, through the bushes and trees, to the closest bathhouse. It was a testament to how worried she was about Poppy that she didn't say a single word about how she'd never been camping in her life. Under any other circumstances, she'd have pitched an epic hissy fit at the very idea of a communal shower.

When we got back, everyone, including Beverly and Frankie, was gathered on the patio at Mamma and Daddy's cottage. Mamma, Beverly, and Frankie had a little group hug, then Mamma collapsed into an Adirondack chair between Beverly and Daddy. Mamma reached for his hand. He clasped hers in both of his.

Normally in a family crisis, Daddy was in charge. He was accustomed to calling the shots. But he was out of his element, and he was wise enough to know it. He was in an unfamiliar place where they drove on the wrong side of the road. His posse of Southern good-ole-boys was far away. He was likely still processing the information about Nate's inheritance, the fact that Bart's job was actually security, and that he had a team of four more people somewhere on the island.

Nate said, "Liz and I are going over to the restaurant so we can use the Wi-Fi. There's not any here in the cottages, and we didn't bring much with us on vacation in the way of equipment. Thankfully, we do have our laptops. We need to figure out who would want to kill Melvin Baker. Because whoever did that is desperate to hide it, and they've taken Poppy to that end. When we find Mr. Baker's killer, we will find Poppy. Bart's going to stay here just in case. Blake?"

Blake nodded. "I'll come along with y'all. I don't have a laptop with me, but I know how you two work. I want to be there when you start formulating a plan."

"Let's go then," I said.

Using our phones for light, the three of us hustled down the path to the Raintree Cafe, which was a large covered deck with vaulted ceilings, skylights, and ceiling fans. A chalkboard near the kitchen advertised the daily specials they'd stopped serving at eight.

It was only eight fifteen, but perhaps because it was Christmas Eve, we had the place to ourselves. We set up on a four-top table near the perimeter. The open-air restaurant was surrounded by trees and all manner of tropical foliage. Nate and I pulled our laptops out of our backpacks and powered them up. There was little to go on, and no reason to suspect anyone had followed Melvin to St. John in order to kill him. Whatever led to Melvin's death had happened here.

I opened a case file. "I'll take Starla Douglas," I said. "I think the mini blind king of Ohio had a pretty sedate life until he met her."

"As you wish," said Nate. "I'll do a deep dive on Melvin Baker."

Blake leaned forward, his elbows on his knees, and prayed while we worked.

Ten minutes in, I found something. "Starla Douglas has a history here on St. John." I clicked back and forth between two of our subscription databases, filling Nate and Blake in. "She moved here from Ohio three years ago and has only been back in Twinsburg a little more than a year. Looks like she worked three jobs, more or less simultaneously: one as a tour guide on the petroglyph hike, one as a waitress at the Lime Inn, and one at Big Planet—the store at Mongoose junction. I'm going to take a look at her social media activity."

Starla was twenty-three. More people in her age group used Instagram than Facebook. I searched, hoping her account wasn't private. There ... her last post was a selfie from the beach in front of the Westin earlier that day. Good grief. Was that bikini even legal here?

I scrolled backwards. There were only three photos posted from this trip, both of the others beach shots.

Most everything recent was yoga related. I kept scrolling until the photos once again featured St. John vistas, then I slowed the scroll.

The feed from three years ago included beaches, sailboats, and local St. John restaurants and bars. And a handsome young man of roughly Starla's age.

"Y'all, look at this." I slid my computer around. "That guy look familiar to you?"

"That's the bartender who was hassling Starla at Jolly Mon Grill last night," said Nate.

Blake scowled at the picture. "You think this guy took Poppy?"

"I don't know yet," I said. "But his name is Ryan Green, and I plan to ask him."

I pulled a profile on Ryan Green. "He's originally from Fort Wayne, Indiana," I said. "He's lived here a little more than five years. This is odd..."

"What?" asked Blake.

"Unlike most people who live here, he only has the one job. Tending bar at Jolly Mon Grill must pay very well."

"Or he has other jobs off the books," said Nate. "Melvin and Beverly's lives were an open book. I say we stick together and focus on Ryan."

Just then, my phone sang out the pinball ringtone, indicating a caller not in my contacts. It was from a blocked number.

"Best answer," said Nate.

"Put it on speaker," said Blake.

I nodded, answered, and hit the speaker button.

"You're not at the airport." A man's voice, probably younger, possibly Black.

"We've decided to wait for Poppy," I said.

"You don't get to decide," said the caller. "If you ever want to see L'il Mamma again, you'd best be on your way."

"We have no guarantee whatsoever we'll ever see her again, even if we do everything you say to the letter," I said.

"And yet, that's your only choice."

"We'll send you the money now as a show of good faith," said Nate. "Then you return Poppy to us unharmed, and we'll all leave together when we've finished our vacation. And since none of us have ever met Melvin Baker, it'll be real easy for us to forget all about him."

"You want me to believe you have a million dollars on you?"

"I'll have the money wired," said Nate.

"On Christmas Eve?"

The man on the phone was right. Unless Nate had that much cash buried in mayonnaise jars in the backyard at Cinnamon Ridge, or in the Deepfreeze in the utility room on the lower level, our financial hands were tied through the holiday.

"See what you can do," said the caller. "Maybe scrape

together a nice down payment. Cash. I'll get back with you." He ended the call.

"How'd they get my number?" I wondered. "It had to be from Poppy. But why would they call me instead of Blake or you?"

"Can't they track your location now through your phone?" asked Blake.

"It depends on who we're dealing with," said Nate. "We've installed utilities that should prevent that unless we're dealing with law enforcement or someone with better-than-typical technical skills. But not answering the call seemed like a worse option in the circumstances."

Blake nodded. "You're right. What now?"

I searched Ryan Green in St. John and came up with an address in Cruz Bay.

"Now we go talk to Ryan Green," I said.

Chapter Eleven

Ryan Green lived in an apartment near Mongoose Junction, the closest thing St. John had to a mall. Filled with shops and restaurants designed to appeal to tourists, it was a stone's throw from Jolly Mon Grill. The small apartment complex was a strip that held maybe a dozen one-level apartments. Ryan's was on the end farthest from the street.

"What if I knock on the door and ask politely?" I asked.

"Sounds good," said Nate. "Blake, would you slip around to the patio in case he pulls a runner and tries to bolt out the back? I'll hang around out here in case Mr. Green is less than courteous to Liz."

"Roger that," said Blake.

We gave him a few minutes to get into place. Nate called me, and I answered and left the call open on my phone so he could hear. Then I approached the front door and rang the bell.

Presently, Ryan Green himself opened the door more than a crack, but not exactly wide open like he had nothing to hide. Ryan had likely been too handsome for his own good his entire life.

"Can I help you?" He was trying real hard to sound casual.

"Gosh, I sure hope so." I offered him a sad smile. "I'm looking for my sister-in-law."

Ryan shrugged, gave me an innocent look. "You think she's here?"

"Maybe," I said, "but I doubt it."

"What makes you think I'd have any idea where your sister-in-law is? I don't know either one of you."

"It's a long story." I turned the volume all the way up on my Southern charm. "Think I could come in and explain?"

Ryan shrugged. "Okay, sure." He looked up and down the street, then stepped back to let me in. "Place is kind of a mess. Have a seat." He moved a blanket and a sweatshirt, clearing a spot on the sofa. The kitchen was open to the living area. A closed door on the far end of the room likely led to a bedroom.

I took the seat he indicated, and he sat in the recliner.

"I have no idea why you'd think your sister-in-law would be here," he said. "But as you can see, I'm alone."

I nodded. "Normally, I would take this very slowly

with you, maybe trick you into telling me what I need to know. I'm a private investigator, and I'm really good at my job. But today, I purely don't have time for the niceties. So tell me, where can I find Starla Douglas?"

He looked confused. "Star's your sister-in-law? I thought she was an only child... I know she's not married. Well, I'm pretty sure of it, anyhow."

I nodded, just as agreeable as I could be. "You're right. She is an only child. And she's not married. But she came here with a man—Melvin Baker—you met him last night at Jolly Mon Grill? Sadly, Melvin has met with foul play. And whoever is responsible has kidnapped my sister-in-law. Star, as you call her, is nowhere to be found."

Ryan paled. "What? Back up. *What* happened? Why would they do that? What does your sister-in-law have to do with this Melvin? What does Star have to do with any of this?"

"All excellent questions," I said. "Where is Starla?"

"Last I heard, she was at the Westin with her new sugar daddy."

I rolled my lips in, shook my head. "I don't think that's true. And here's why. I think Starla saw something that scared her, so she ran away. And where else would she run but to her former boyfriend? You obviously still have feelings for her. That much was clear last night in the restaurant."

He shook his head, gave me a wide eyed look. "I may still care about Starla, I'll give you that much. It bothers me to see her with that old man. But the rest ... I've got no idea what you're talking about."

"Are you certain?" I asked. "Because here's what I'm thinking ... the people who took my sister-in-law, they want me and my family to stay quiet about what we know about Melvin Baker. And the thing is? We don't know him at all. Never met him. In fact, all we really know about him is that he had dinner last night with Starla. So, if they are kidnapping innocent bystanders to keep us quiet, what are they going to do to poor Starla?"

Now I could see stark fear in his eyes. He looked away, then back, and shrugged. "I wish I could help you find your sister-in-law, but I have no idea who took her or why, and I haven't heard from Star. None of this has anything to do with me."

I stood and handed him my business card. "If you hear from her, please ask her to call me. It could easily be a matter of life and death. Perhaps hers."

When we were all back in the Jeep, Blake said, "That Starla chick is hiding in the bedroom. I saw her through the window."

"I'm not surprised," I said. "We need to get a GPS unit on his car, lickety-split."

"Agreed," said Nate. "That's his Kia in front of the apartment. I ran the tags."

Blake wore a confused look. "Why do you need to track him? Why not just go back in there and demand to talk to the girl hiding in his bedroom?"

I said, "If Ryan knows who has Poppy, or suspects he does, and if Starla is in danger because of something to do with all this—and of course she is—Ryan is going to leave soon and go try to negotiate her safety. We need to follow him.

"As you probably noticed, St. John is not an island easily navigated. There are only a few main roads, but they are full of hairpin turns and steep climbs and drop-offs. It's too easy for someone to turn down a dirt road or a driveway and disappear. We have to be able to track Ryan. But we didn't bring GPS trackers on vacation. We can use one of our phones, as long as location services are set right, but Nate has to have his in case Bart or someone else from the team tries to reach him. The kidnappers called us on my phone, so we can't risk using it as a tracker. The only option is to use your phone. If we can somehow get it attached to Ryan's car, we can trace his movements."

"What if Poppy tries to call me?" he asked.

"She'll call one of us if she can't reach you," I said. "Look, it's not perfect, but we really need to do this."

"All right, fine."

I put his phone in silent mode, downloaded our tracking app of choice, set location services, and checked the battery. "You're at sixty-five percent battery life. Hopefully, that will be enough."

Nate pulled the magnetic phone holder off the dash. "It's a good thing we bought the high-powered magnets. Be right back. Create a distraction if you need to."

He slipped out of the Jeep. Leaving the door open, he crouched and crept over to Ryan's car. He bent down and attached Blake's phone inside Ryan's wheel well, then hustled back to the car and climbed in, easing the door closed behind him.

Nate drove the Jeep out of the parking lot and down the street a ways. Then he pulled into a parking spot in front of Mongoose Junction. A high percentage of the cars on the island were some flavor of Jeep. It was easy to blend in.

"I wish we had binoculars," I said. "I'm never traveling without equipment again."

Nate looked at me with an expression I couldn't decipher.

"What?" I asked.

"Slugger, my plan is to never need this kind of equipment again. And if I hadn't been trying to be discreet, keep the money thing quiet, we would've been traveling with more security than just Bart. This would never have happened."

"There is no way any of this is your fault," I said.

"Maybe not," said Nate, "but you can be damned sure of one thing. I will take better care of all of us every next time that comes."

Chapter Twelve

We didn't have long to wait. Five minutes later, Ryan tore past us on North Shore Road. Nate let one car go between us, then backed into the street, turned, and followed Ryan. "You got him?"

The blue dot on the tracking app was strong. "Yes. He's turning left on Highway 10."

"No sign of Starla," said Blake. "Either he's left her back at the apartment or she's hiding in the floorboard."

"I'm betting he left her there," I said. "It's safer."

We followed him over Bordeaux Mountain, all the way across the island to Coral Bay. Then he took a right turn on a winding dirt road and headed up into the hills, to parts of St. John Nate and I had never seen before.

The blue dot on the map flashed red and stopped moving. "We've lost cell signal," I said.

"Well, we're unlikely to lose him on this road," said

Nate. "Neither of us can go more than ten miles an hour."
He pulled closer to Ryan, keeping his taillights in view.

The night got even darker, with dense woods closing
in on both sides of the Jeep. Finally, Ryan pulled into a
dirt driveway. We drove on past a ways, cut the lights and
parked. The tree frogs, birds, and all manner of critters
sang a symphony all around us.

"We are in the damn jungle," said Blake.

"I have no idea where we are," I said. "I think there
was a sign on that tree. I'm going to take a closer look."

Nate killed the overhead light. "Be careful."

Stepping carefully over uneven terrain, tree roots, and
rocks, I made my way to the tree and shined the flashlight
on my cell phone in the general area where I'd glimpsed a
sign.

It was hand painted, in uneven blue letters: "Tourist
Information: You are lost."

I climbed back into the Jeep and reported what I'd
found.

"I'm going to take a look around," said Nate. "Would
y'all mind staying here in case I need you to turn on the
lights so I can find my way back?"

I raised an eyebrow at my husband. He wanted me to
stay in the car where it was relatively safe.

"It's too dark for me to see that eyebrow climb your
forehead," he said. "But, seriously, one of us needs to see
what's going on inside. We can't risk all of us going."

"You think Poppy's in there?" asked Blake.

"I don't know," said Nate. "I hope so."

"I'm going with you," said Blake.

"I figured as much," said Nate. "Liz, I know this is against your nature, but will you please stay in the car?"

"I can't," I said. "Don't ask me to do that. We don't know who these people are or what they're capable of. We need to stick together and back each other up."

"I can't believe I'm saying this, but I think she's right," said Blake. "Our best chance of all of us going home alive is staying together."

"Let's get this done then." Nate's voice was tense.

As quietly as we could, we got out of the Jeep and negotiated our way back down to where Ryan had turned in. We crouched behind the thick, twisty trunk of a tamarind tree, its feathery leaves drooping to offer us coverage. A metal building surrounded by a high fence sat back off the road. We watched and waited less than five minutes.

"Someone's coming." It was so dark, I could only make out his outline. Then Ryan came into focus. He bounded back to the car, got in, and started the engine.

Blake said, "Pick me up on the way back by. I see a sign. I want to know what this place is."

"Roger that," said Nate.

"I hope it's more helpful than the sign on the tree," I said.

Nate and I made our way back to the car. He executed

a five-point turn, and we rolled to a stop at the end of the driveway. Blake hopped in.

"St. John Auto Salvage," he said. "There's junk cars inside the fence. Looks like they're taking them apart."

Nate accelerated. "Hopefully, we'll get cell service again in a minute. If Ryan didn't find who he was looking for here, maybe he knows where else to look."

Chapter Thirteen

Next we followed Ryan to a laundromat, then to a vending machine company, both in Coral Bay. Whoever he was looking for evidently wasn't in either place. He was in and out lickety-split. Then we followed him out East End Road to Hansen Bay Beach, one of the most remote spots on the island. Ryan pulled into a dirt parking lot, and Nate cut the lights on the Jeep and pulled to the side of the road a ways back. We all got out and slunk along the side of the road, then crouched and waddled up to a clump of trees. This part of the island wasn't as densely covered in greenery. We could see much more by the light of the moon than we could on the hillside.

"There's nothing out here," said Blake. "Maybe he's meeting someone."

"There's something here," said Nate. "See that?" He pointed.

"It looks like a floating shipping container," said Blake. The bright pink box with blue, green, and yellow sea creatures painted on the sides was moored just off the beach.

"That's Jammin'," said Nate. "It's a floating restaurant —similar to a food truck. Aunt Odella owns it. When it's open, you have to take a boat or a paddleboard or an inner tube—some sort of watercraft—out to it. They serve tacos, sandwiches, fries, nachos, and more liquor than a bunch of Tennessee moonshiners. Food here is every bit as good as her brisket. It would appear someone's operating an after-hours sideline enterprise."

"I think there's someone on board," I said. The service windows were pulled closed, but a thin bead of light emitted from around the edges.

Ryan walked into the water. It was only waist deep when he pulled himself up onto the deck surrounding the building. Then he walked around to the other side, putting the restaurant between us.

After five minutes passed, I said, "He's stayed here longer than anywhere. He must've found who he was looking for."

"I'm going in," said Blake.

"No way you'll climb aboard without them hearing you," I said. "Ryan knows whoever's inside, maybe called ahead. I doubt they're feeling hospitable this evening."

"You got a plan?" There was a challenge in my brother's voice.

"I'm working on one." I mulled things a bit further. "I'll swim up to the far side and ask about ordering a drink, act a little drunk. While I'm engaging the occupants, the two of you climb aboard, from different ends. There can't be more than two or three people in there. With kitchen equipment and all, it's got to be small inside."

"Good plan," said Nate. "But since Ryan has met you, I'll play the part of the drunk attempting to place an order. Also, you're hardly dressed for the occasion."

I glanced down. I was wearing head-to-toe Christmas Eve winter white. An Ellen Tracy short-sleeved popover sweater above matching capris. Fabrics so delicate, I was barely wearing anything beneath them. But this outfit would definitely make swimming difficult. And with that thought, I was out of my sweater in one movement, dropping it at my feet.

"Aw, come on, *seriously?*" My brother covered his eyes.

We stood close enough together I could read my husband's expression. He purely did not care for this plan.

Before he could verbalize his objections, I said, "My hair will be wet. It's dark out. And I'll be in vastly different attire than the last time Ryan laid eyes on me. I seriously doubt he'll recognize me. And why would it matter anyway? As soon as you two climb aboard, they're going to know I'm up to something. All I'm trying to do is buy the two of you a few extra seconds."

By then, I was out of my capris.

To Nate I said, "I'm wearing way more bikini than Starla was wearing in the picture we saw," and to my brother, I said, "grow up."

Blake uncovered his eyes and looked everywhere but at me. "You know I hate it when she's right, but I think it's better for the two of us to be on board and her in the water."

"I'll take the left side," said Nate. "Let's do this."

We crossed the parking lot in a crouched run.

As quietly as I could, I slid into the water, fervently hoping my La Perla ivory unmentionables would stay in place. I swam along the sandy bottom underneath the barge. As I broke the surface on the other side, I saw what we'd missed from the shore: a boat—a silver and black Fountain powerboat, low and sleek. This was what they typically used to pull Jammin' around Hansen Bay and out into the larger Coral Bay. A grey rubber dinghy was tethered behind it.

I slicked my hair back, got my bearings, and swam up to the deck that ran around the perimeter of what looked like an old shipping container for the simple reason that's exactly what it was.

The deck was deserted. From this side of the restaurant, I couldn't see any more than I could from shore. There were lights on inside. But I could hear voices. Men arguing. I couldn't make out what they were saying, but it was heated.

I grabbed the side of the deck and pulled myself up far

enough to hook my arms over the side. I knew the guys would be in place by now. They'd only had to wade into the water as we'd watched Ryan do.

"*Yoo-hoo,*" I called. "Anybody home? I'd like a margarita on the rocks, please."

The door opened, and a very tall, very brawny man appeared. He took in my bare shoulders and prowled closer, looking intrigued. I recognized that walk. He had to be one of the men who'd been following Melvin and Starla after dinner last night. *Damnation.* Well, we were likely at the right place anyway.

"Do you know what time it is?" he asked, a bit of a tease in his voice. "Do you know it's Christmas Eve? We're closed." He pointed to the posted hours. "We open again day after tomorrow."

"But I seriously need a margarita. Are you sure you couldn't help a girl out?" I offered him a sunny smile.

A conflicted expression flitted across his face as he considered the situation.

Then a splash came from the far side of one end of the deck, then the other.

Brawny Man scowled, advancing out of the doorway. "Devon, get out here."

Devon came through the door.

Brawny Man nodded right. "We got company."

They moved towards opposite ends of the barge. Brawny man glowered at me over his shoulder.

Then, everything happened at once.

Ryan bolted from the restaurant and took a running leap into the water.

Devon cursed loudly, spun, and jumped in after him. He was on top of him instantly. The two of them wrestled in the water, thrashing and splashing.

Brawny Man watched them for a second, then tilted his head and advanced towards me with ominous intent.

Nate grabbed his arm from behind, spun him around, and shoved him hard into the water.

I pulled myself up onto the deck.

Blake rounded the end of the restaurant and poked his head through the door.

Nate grabbed me by the shoulders, looked me up and down to make sure I was okay. Then we both moved towards the door of the restaurant.

Blake shook his head. "She's not here. No one else is here."

The sloshing noises from the battle in the water dissipated.

We all turned our attention to the bay.

Brawny Man pulled himself up the ladder onto the boat.

Devon surfaced and swam towards the craft, then hoisted himself up.

The engine started.

Seconds later, the boat darted out into Coral Bay, then disappeared around Ram Head.

The engine misfired. *Chug-chug-gasp-chug.*

"That's got to be the same boat," said Nate.

"I don't see Ryan." My eyes scanned the bay.

"There." Nate pointed, then dove into the water.

Ryan floated face down thirty feet away.

Nate reached him in a few strong strokes, then towed him to shore. Blake and I jumped off the back of the barge and waded to the beach.

Nate pulled Ryan onto the sand. I called St. John Rescue. We took turns performing CPR, trying to revive him until the ambulance arrived. The EMTs took in the scene as they dashed across the sand. My attire didn't give them a second's pause. They'd likely seen all manner of situations.

We backed out of the way to let them do their jobs.

A female toting heavy satchels called over her shoulder to me, "There are hospital gowns in our unit. Maybe even a T-shirt. What's his status?"

Nate said, "We pulled him out of the water about thirty minutes ago and started CPR right away."

I moved towards the ambulance and dug around for anything to put on. The police hadn't arrived. Had the rescue team called them? Things worked differently in St. John than on the U.S. mainland. St. John Rescue was an all-volunteer organization.

"We've done all we can for him." I pulled an extra-large Skinny Legs long-sleeved hoodie over my head.

"He's gone," said Blake. "It goes against every fiber of my grain to leave before the police get here, but if we wait, we'll be tied up here for hours—possibly days. We'll never find Poppy in time."

"He's right," said Nate. "When we're far enough away, we can call it in, make sure someone knows foul play was involved here. But we can't wait."

I grabbed my discarded clothes, and we ran back to the Jeep. I was too wet to put my nice things back on. As we sped away into the night, a cauldron of emotions swirled inside me. I was sick with worry for Poppy. But I struggled mightily with leaving that poor soul on the beach. He might've been involved with shady characters, and maybe he did lie to us. But just like us, he'd been trying to save someone he cared about that night.

Chapter Fourteen

~∞~

We headed back out East End Road, which becomes Centerline in the town of Coral Bay. Nate focused on driving. The twisting, climbing roads of St. John demanded your full attention in broad daylight. At night they were especially treacherous. The wandering goats, deer, and donkeys didn't wear reflective gear.

Instead of following Centerline all the way back to Cruz Bay, we turned right on North Shore Road, which cut across the island. After a hairpin turn or two, North Shore made a hard left at Maho Bay, then followed the coastline. We were back at Cinnamon Bay in record time.

Along the way, in addition to calling the police—after blocking my number via the feature built into the phone as well as a handy piece of software we utilized when necessary for extra security—I called Bart and asked him to have Starla Douglas escorted from Ryan Green's apartment to the campground. There was no doubt in my mind that she was the hoodlums' next target.

"Are you sure she's in his apartment?" Bart asked.

"She was earlier. She has nowhere else to go, plus she's scared out of her mind, so I'd say it's a safe bet."

"Does she know one of us is coming? Did you give her an all-clear password?" he asked.

"No, she doesn't, and no, I didn't. I don't have a way to reach her. But if she wants reassurance as to who sent our guy, have him tell her I was there earlier, I know she was hiding in the bedroom listening, and I know Ryan calls her Star. Tell him to say we have a message from Ryan." That was true in a way, I supposed. He would want us to keep her safe.

Ryan had clearly tried to negotiate on Starla's behalf. That effort caused him to wind up dead. The first place they'd look for her would be his apartment. We had to make sure they didn't find her.

As soon as we'd parked in the lot, I zipped into the restroom, did my best to finish drying off with paper towels, and slipped my clothes back on. If I'd had more time, I'd've found something more appropriate for the venue. My Christmas Eve outfit would have to do. I joined Nate and Blake in the restaurant, where they'd settled back in at our previous table.

"The fact the kidnappers haven't called back is not a

good sign." Blake wore a haggard look. "Those two thugs knew exactly who we were, which is the only reason they didn't kill us. They haven't gotten their money yet."

"I'm afraid you're right," said Nate. "They're clearly in cahoots with whoever took Poppy. And obviously, they now know we're actively hunting them."

"We were," said Blake. "The trail died with Ryan Green, didn't it?"

"No," I said. "Starla knows everything he knew, probably more. We just have to convince her it's in her best interest to share what she knows. She should be here shortly. Provided whoever Bart sent was able to convince her to trust him."

"Do you figure Ryan knew about the kidnapping before you mentioned it to him?" Nate asked.

"No." I shook my head. "I'm nearly certain he didn't."

In the middle of the night, the campground was eerily quiet. The sound of a car pulling up, and the door opening and closing, carried across the parking lot and onto the deck that was the restaurant.

"That's most likely Starla now," said Nate. "Be right back."

He returned moments later with a very frightened-looking Starla. He made the introductions.

"You all were in the restaurant last night." She turned to me. "And you were at Ryan's earlier. The guy who dropped me off said you had a message from Ryan? I figured that was probably a trick, but ... my options are limited right now. Do you? Have a message from Ryan?" Her eyes held both fear and hope.

Nate pulled another of the white plastic chairs to our table. "Maybe you should have a seat."

Reluctantly, Starla sat. She looked more like a scared kid than a femme fatale. How had she gotten mixed up in all of this?

I reached out and rubbed her arm. "I'm afraid I have sad news. It's not really my place to tell you this, and ordinarily, I wouldn't. But I'm afraid your life may depend on you knowing what I'm about to tell you." I drew a deep breath and let it out. "Ryan is dead."

She made a whimpering noise and brought both her hands to her mouth, then shook her head. "Oh no ... please." She cried and shook and rocked back and forth.

We gave her a few minutes. I continued to rub her arm.

"What happened?" she asked eventually.

Nate said, "He had an altercation with two miscreants over at Jammin'." He gave her the broad strokes of what had happened, descriptions of the men, and the fact that one of them was named Devon. "These same two men were following you and Mr. Baker last night. Do you know who they are?"

"I didn't know they were following us last night," she said. "Devon—that has to be Devon Keeler. Which means

the other is Marcus Callwood. You'll rarely see one
without the other. All I knew about either of them up
until last night was that they were Ryan's friends."

"Not so much, as it turns out," I said. "What
happened last night?"

"Well, as you know, Melvin and I had dinner at Jolly
Mon Grill. Ryan and I—we have history. I lived here for a
while. We dated. I guess it's fair to say he was more
attached than I was. Anyway, St. John is magical, but it's
really hard to make a living here. I moved back to Ohio.
That's where I met Melvin."

She teared up, sobbed again, then continued. "Melvin
was such a sweetheart. I know what you must think, him
being so much older and all. But he was really good to me.
I told him all about St. John, and how much I loved it
here. He surprised me with this trip. Honestly, I could
never tell him this, but I didn't want to come back here at
all."

I felt my face scrunch. "Why not? I thought you said
you loved it here?"

She winced. "Ryan was a bit persistent. It's a small
island. I knew we'd run into him. I wanted a fresh start
with Melvin, I guess, free from everything from my past."

Just then I was wondering how she planned on having
a fresh start with a married man, and what she thought
about *his* past, and the wife he'd tossed aside, but I didn't
interrupt.

"And of course, we did run into him at Jolly Mon last

night. Melvin insisted we eat there. He'd read all the wonderful reviews. Wednesday was Ryan's night off for years, so I thought it would be safe, but I guess he switched with someone, or maybe he needed the hours. The hostess seated us directly in front of the bar, where he couldn't possibly have missed us. I was physically ill.

"As soon as Melvin went to the men's room, Ryan was all up in my face making horribly mean comments about me having a sugar daddy. It wasn't like that with Melvin and me. I'm a business owner. Anyway, Melvin saw us arguing—saw Ryan grab my arm. I guess Ryan didn't want to get fired for having an altercation with a customer, so he went into the kitchen—well, I always thought that was the kitchen. I don't know what all is back there now. Melvin followed him. He was so mad.

"And when he came back out, Melvin said...." She hesitated, swallowed hard. "He *said* Ryan went into an office in the back and closed the door behind him. When Melvin opened the door and went in after him, he saw a woman counting a suitcase full of money. He backed out and shut the door fast. But when he turned around, down a dark hallway, he saw two men moving a body out of the freezer."

We all stared at her.

"Melvin wasn't the kind to make things up," she said. "He was a straight arrow. But I thought he'd just misinterpreted things ... maybe they were moving a side of beef—it is a restaurant, after all. And the money ... who knows?

But it wasn't our business. It spooked Melvin, but I guess I convinced him to let it go—that he hadn't seen what he thought he did. And I cost him his life. And now Ryan's too." She dissolved into tears.

"Starla," I said gently, "I'm so sorry for your loss—both your losses. But in the interest of keeping you alive ... and there are other lives in the balance as well ... please tell us what happened to Melvin. Did you see Marcus and Devon kill him? Is that why they're after you?"

"This evening we went to Virgin Bistro for an early dinner." She wiped a tear from her eye. "It was so romantic. I thought he was going to propose. Then, I thought, maybe he would do it later. It was a perfect evening, right up until the nightmare started."

She teared up, took a moment to compose herself, and then continued. "We went for a walk on the beach. Then we sat in the lounge chairs along the water and watched the sunset. I needed a sweater, and Melvin went to the room to get me one. As soon as he left, a dinghy motored to shore. Marcus and Devon got out and pulled it up onto the sand. I didn't think too much about it at first.

"When Melvin didn't come back, I went to look for him and found him dead on the floor by the bed. I knew right away he'd really seen what he said he saw. And I figured they'd know he would've possibly told *me* what he saw. And maybe they'd seen me outside—they'd know that I saw them in the dinghy. I was certain I was on their hit list. I was terrified. I didn't know where they'd gone or if they were coming back. I grabbed all my things and ran out the patio doors. I went around the side of the building and ran across the lawn and hid in some trees near the little gazebo by the water. I don't know how long I was there trying to figure out some kind of plan.

"But then I saw Marcus and Devon carrying what must've been poor Melvin wrapped in a tarp, or a blanket, across the beach. They put him in the dinghy. I think they must've been in a larger boat. I heard one start and leave the bay right after that."

Nate and I exchanged a glance. Starla had been hiding in the gazebo while we went inside Melvin's room.

"Then what did you do?" I asked.

"I called Ryan. There's a road that runs along the far side of the tennis courts back to near where the gazebo sits. He picked me up and took me back to his apartment."

"You weren't afraid of him?" Blake asked. "He was their friend you said."

"He thought they were his friends, anyway," said Starla. "But I was counting on him still being a little bit in love with me. I think he must've been. And that got him killed." Tears rolled down her cheeks.

"I wonder where they went," I said. "After they killed Melvin, and before they moved the body … seems like an odd time for a coffee break."

"It does indeed." Nate frowned.

We all mulled that for a minute, then I had an idea.

"What if they had to leave for the same reason Beverly and Frankie had to climb the hill earlier? They had to make a call and couldn't get cell signal?"

Nate nodded. "That would make sense."

"Who are Beverly and Frankie?" Starla asked.

Nate and I exchanged a glance. Did she really not know?

"We'll come back to them in just a minute," said Nate. "You said Ryan was friends with Marcus and Devon."

"They were his first friends when he moved here from Fort Wayne, Indiana," said Starla.

"What do they do for a living?" I asked.

"They work for St. John Auto Salvage," said Starla. "They buy junk cars and take them apart. They sell a lot of the parts locally for repairs. Then they crush what's left and ship the scrap metal somewhere for recycling."

"Who owns that place?" I asked.

Starla shrugged. "I have no idea. Not Marcus or Devon. They just work there. But there was something I heard ... I don't know if you've noticed, but there are quite a few cars on the island that aren't fully operational. Whoever owns the salvage yard had a plan ... there was some sort of grant involved, I think. The idea was to convince local authorities to ticket people for hanging onto cars that wouldn't run. That would've meant revenue for the local government and a lot more business for the salvage yard. But I don't think they ever got the local authorities to buy into it."

I opened my laptop. "If Devon and Marcus needed to make a call in the middle of a crime, it was no doubt for instructions. I'm thinking it's likely they are hired muscle for someone else—not the folks who call the shots. And someone else had to've taken Poppy. We got the call that she was missing before Devon and Marcus could possibly have reached the house."

"They've kidnapped someone too?" asked Starla.

"My wife," said Blake.

"I don't understand any of this," said Starla.

"So you didn't know about the kidnapping?" I asked. "I couldn't see how you could've before Ryan picked you up. But Ryan didn't mention it?"

"Not until after you left," said Starla. "He was frantic. Ryan wouldn't be involved in kidnappings and killings. I said I thought Marcus and Devon were his friends. And clearly, I know now they're criminals. Ryan was *not*."

"As far as you know," said Blake. "But you said he walked into the office where the woman was counting the suitcase full of money."

"That does seem to point to him being involved in some sort of criminal activity," I said.

"It's possible he earned extra money doing odd jobs around the salvage yard," said Starla. "And I suppose it's *possible* not everything that goes on there is strictly legal. But Ryan was a gentle soul. He'd never hurt anyone."

"What do you think they might be up to that isn't strictly legal?" I asked.

"I have no idea," said Starla.

"Then why do you think not everything that goes on there is legal?" asked Nate.

Starla shrugged and stared at something over Nate's shoulder. "Ryan was sort of secretive about it. At first, I just thought it was because they were paying him under the table. But maybe there was more to it. I just can't believe they killed him."

I opened a subscription database and searched St. John Auto Salvage. "St. John Auto Savage is owned by another company, St. John Investments ... and that is owned by Consolidated St. John Enterprises. This could take a while to sort out."

Time was the one thing we purely did not have.

I said, "I think what we have here is a chain reaction of events that started when Melvin saw something he shouldn't have in the back at Jolly Mon Grill. Whatever he saw got him killed, and during the killing, Starla saw something she shouldn't have, and then the killers saw us going into Melvin's room. They called someone who then grabbed Poppy. But how did they know who we were and where we were staying?"

"A fair assessment and a good question." Nate turned to Starla. "Is there anything else you can tell us that might help us find my sister-in-law?"

"Nothing I'm aware of," she said.

Nate's phone rang. He had a short conversation, then

ended the call. "That was Bart. Starla, I hope you'll stay here with us until we know everyone is safe."

"That's awfully kind of you," she said. "I don't have anywhere else to go."

"They didn't have another cottage available," said Nate, "but they've put you in another section, in an eco-tent—it's like a tent on a platform. Probably best if you're not right next to the rest of our party anyway. Hopefully, it's just for tonight."

She wore a confused expression. "Thank you—truly. I'm grateful."

"Perhaps you'd like some time to yourself?" asked Nate. "I can walk you over there. As soon as we've figured out the next steps, we'll let you know."

As she started to stand, I asked the question that had been bugging me, out of pure-T curiosity, "How did you figure Melvin was going to propose to you? I didn't think polygamy was legal in Ohio."

"What?" She leaned in, tilted her head, bewilderment washing over her face.

"Melvin hasn't even separated from his first wife, let alone divorced her," I said.

She straightened, looked indignant. "Melvin was a widower."

"Is that what he told you?" I asked.

"It's the truth," she insisted. "His first wife died in a terrible car accident five years ago. He's been alone ever since. Well, except for his kids, of course."

I couldn't help but feel sorry for her. "I'm afraid that's not the case. The only reason we were even in that restaurant last night was because my mamma befriended Melvin's wife, who followed y'all here. I expect she would've divorced him as quickly as possible, but they were still married and still living in the same house when he died."

She sat down hard on the chair. "I just can't believe that."

"Did you ever go to his house?" I asked.

"Well, no ... his daughter lives with him. She's got some emotional issues ... has never really gotten over her mother's death. We spent time together in my apartment to avoid upsetting her."

I nodded. "Ever meet any of his friends? Other family?"

She shook her head slowly.

"Did he take you out a lot? To restaurants? Movies? That sort of thing?"

"No, Melvin always said my cooking was better than any restaurant. He never really liked restaurants. Said you never knew what they put in your food." Her forehead creased in confusion. "Though he really enjoyed eating out here."

I was reasonably certain the reason Melvin had an aversion to restaurants in the Twinsburg, Ohio, area was because his wife was a food blogger and well known in foodie circles there.

"Ever go by his office for any reason?" I asked.

"No," she said softly, staring down at the deck. "I am such a fool."

Nate offered her an arm. "Let's get you to your tent so you can have some time to yourself."

Chapter Fifteen

I was determined to find out who Marcus and Devon worked for. While Nate escorted Starla to her eco-tent, I scoured every database I could think of. Whoever owned St. John Auto Salvage had taken great pains to conceal their identity.

"I can't just sit here another minute." Blake stood.

"We can't go door-to-door looking for her, either," I said.

"Hell I can't. They have my wife. And my child."

"I know," I said. "And—wait..."

"What?"

"The kidnappers ... on the phone, they referred to Poppy as 'L'il Mamma'. Poppy's not even showing yet. How did they know she was pregnant?"

Blake's eyes cut to the right, his expression signifying he was thinking hard. "Maybe she told them?"

I shook my head. "I don't think she'd do that. Her instincts would be to protect the baby."

Nate walked back across the deck. Antsy, he didn't sit, but put his hands on the back of one of the white plastic chairs and gripped.

"How did the kidnappers know Poppy was expecting?" I asked. "They called her 'L'il Mamma'. It didn't register with me before. It's not the kind of information she'd offer."

He squinted at me. "It's a puzzlement how they even knew who we were or where to look for a family member. The only people we've interacted with since we arrived are the ladies originally from the Upstate and more recently Ryan and Starla."

"And Jenny." Our eyes locked. "What was her last name again?"

"Vanterpool," he said.

I commenced to searching but learned very little. "She's a St. John native. Thirty years old. Operates her own business, We Cater to You."

"I found her through the real estate agent I used to buy this house. That was ... three years ago? She's shopped and cooked for me every time I've been here, but I always book her through them. I just can't imagine she's a party to this."

"She might not be," I said. "But she might've said something to someone, not knowing it was important..."

"Maybe," said Nate. "It's also possible someone overheard something on the beach, or at a restaurant..."

"Mamma does announce to anyone who will listen that Poppy's expecting her first grandchild," I said. "I overheard her telling Beverly and Frankie that—we probably all did. Who all else did she mention it to?"

"There are just not enough dots to connect here," said Blake.

"Let's think about this from another angle," I said. "Melvin saw a woman counting a suitcase full of cash and two men—likely Marcus and Devon—moving a body. There's clearly an underlying, ongoing criminal operation we've stumbled into. St. John Auto Salvage ... they sell car parts, right? And export scrap metal. I wonder what else they export—or import. Ryan also went looking for Marcus and Devon at a laundromat, a vending machine place, and Jammin'. All of these businesses take in a lot of cash."

"You think they're money laundering?" asked Blake.

"Likely among other things," said Nate. "And we know Jammin' is owned by Aunt Odella, as is Aunt Odella's Famous Brisket."

"That doesn't necessarily mean *she's* laundering money," said Blake. "More likely she has a couple employees with second jobs as criminals. She's a grandmother."

"So was Abigail Bounetheau," I said. "And I do have a vivid memory of Mamma telling Aunt Odella all about

Poppy expecting her first grandchild, and them going on and on about grandkids and nurseries and layettes, while the line for brisket got longer and longer and people stared at us in an unfriendly manner."

"If anybody is using those restaurants to launder money, there's no way she doesn't know about it. At a minimum," said Nate.

"I need to find out who owns the laundromat, the vending machine company, and the salvage yard." I turned back to my laptop.

Nate said, "Let me take a turn with the salvage yard. Fresh eyes."

"I'll start with the laundromat," I said.

"I'm going to go ask Starla if Melvin Baker happened to mention what the woman counting the money looked like," said Blake.

Thirty minutes later, Nate said, "She's hidden it well, but Odella Harrigan owns the salvage yard. Have you run across the company name Phoenix Investments?"

"Yes—there are two layers of shell companies before you get to it, but Phoenix Investments owns both the laundromat and the vending machine company."

Blake crossed the deck at a fast clip. "Melvin told Starla the woman counting the money was older with long dreadlocks."

"I'll do a deep dive on Aunt Odella Harrigan." I turned back to my laptop. "I'd be willing to bet my mamma's pearls she owns Jolly Mon Grill."

"What the devil is that?" Blake stared at the skylights.

I followed his gaze to the ceiling. A ghostly, silvery white light floated around the windows in the roof, moved away, then circled back. Nate looked from the ceiling to me, our eyes locking.

Colleen.

We jumped up and bolted out of the restaurant.

Blake followed. "What is that? Was it lightning? The sky is clear."

We dashed down the path and to the center of the parking lot, out from under the canopy of trees. High up on the hill above us, a column of the white, silvery light rose above the trees.

"Where is that?" I asked. "Looks like it's not far from the house."

Nate stared at it another minute. "It's got to be just off Centerline Road. Might be the old Catherineberg sugar plantation ruins?"

"What the devil are we looking at?" asked Blake.

I ran for the Jeep. "It's got nothing to do with the devil. That's an answered prayer. Let's go."

Nate was already opening the driver's door to the Jeep. "Hurry."

Blake stopped asking questions and climbed in.

Chapter Sixteen

We followed North Shore Road to Highway 206—the goat path, as Mamma calls it—and headed up the hill. It was only a mile and a half from the campground to where we thought we were going. But it featured hairpin turns, steep drop-offs, and rugged terrain. It was the longest ten-minute drive of our lives.

The silvery column of white light shrank to what looked like a very large star. Colleen knew we'd seen her, knew we were on our way. She led us straight to the ruins of the Catherineberg sugar plantation.

Nate cut the lights on the Jeep a little ways down the road and rolled into the dirt area that served as a parking lot. Except for us, it was empty. It was too dark to see well, but we'd been here before—and had driven past it many times. It was a tourist attraction, mostly during daylight hours, but no doubt adventurous types—and possibly teenagers—came here at night.

Like other sugar plantation ruins on the island, it was a stone structure featuring the remains of a windmill which had once been used to juice sugar cane, which was then made into sugar and rum. We started with the windmill tower.

"Let's stay with our plan to stick together," said Nate. "This place isn't that big."

I was thinking Colleen would never have led us into danger unless she had no choice whatsoever. And if she'd had to do that, she'd surely stick around to help us out if we needed it. And I was certain Poppy was inside that sugar mill.

I was already out of the car and heading towards the arched entryway.

Blake caught up quickly and passed me.

"Hold up a minute." Nate stopped just inside the building. The area right in front of us had a stone floor, and a few steps led to a raised room with a large center column. Nate shined the flashlight on his phone around the room. It was empty.

"Poppy?" Blake yelled. "You here?"

"*Mmmm, mmmm, mmmmmm.*" It was the urgent call of someone gagged.

"Up top." I darted out the door, and by the light of my phone flashlight, climbed up onto the stone walkway that sloped its way up to the upper level of the tower.

Blake and Nate passed me, hesitated at the doorway, then bolted inside.

"*Poppy.*" Blake's voice was weak with relief.

Poppy was on the stone floor against the wall. "Mmmm, mmmm, mmm."

Blake pulled the rag out of her mouth.

Nate went to work cutting the zip ties that bound her feet and hands.

She coughed, sputtered, and sucked in air. "Jenny."

Blake scooped her up and carried her to the Jeep.

Chapter Seventeen

"Poppy!" Mamma jumped up at the first sight of us and rushed to check her over from head to toe. "Oh, Darlin' I'm just so *relieved*. Blake? Is she all right?"

Everyone gathered around Blake, who still held Poppy in his arms. And everyone was asking the same questions all at once: *Are you all right? What happened? Where did they take you?* et cetera.

"I'm perfectly fine," said Poppy. "Sweetheart, you can put me down now."

"Here." Daddy pointed to the Adirondack chair he'd vacated. "These chairs are the most comfortable. Sit her over here."

Blake eased Poppy into the chair.

"Darlin', we were so worried." Mamma sat beside Poppy, put her hand on her arm, and leaned in. "Tell us everything."

Merry handed Poppy a bottle of water. "Are you sure you're okay?"

"I'm fine. A little sore from sitting on a rock floor for hours. A bit hoarse from the gag. That's it. I feel like a perfect idiot for letting this happen."

"What exactly happened?" asked Mamma.

Poppy had already told us everything on the way back, but she filled the rest of the family in. "Jenny knocked on our bedroom door and asked me if I needed anything. I said no, thank you, but she walked over to the bed and leaned in close, like she was going to check on me. I thought it was a little odd. The next thing you know, she had a cloth over my nose and mouth, and I passed right out. When I came to, I was exactly like they found me—sitting in that old sugar mill with my feet and wrists tied together and a rag in my mouth."

"You never saw anyone aside from Jenny?" asked Bart.

"No." Poppy shook her head.

"Why would anyone take her and just leave her somewhere like that?" Daddy scowled. "Was Jenny mad about something?"

"No, I don't think that was it," said Blake.

"I can't believe that sweet Jenny would do such a thing," said Mamma. "She took such good care of us."

"We're still figuring things out," said Nate. "Bart, where's the rest of the team?"

"Two in Cruz Bay, two in Coral Bay. Digging for leads. Nothing so far."

"Have them head our way," said Nate. "I'm hoping we can catch a boat to St. Thomas at daybreak."

I glanced at my watch. How was it only eleven thirty? Christmas Eve felt like it had lasted a year.

"I'm going to head back to the restaurant," I said. "I've got some work to finish up."

"I'll come with you," said Nate.

"I'm going to hang here, guys. Holler if you need me." Blake had both arms around Poppy's legs.

I laughed. "I don't see you letting go of her anytime soon."

Chapter Eighteen

"Here are the things I don't understand," I said as I dropped into one of the white plastic chairs and scooted it in. "One, how were Marcus and Devon able to wipe everything about Melvin and Starla out of the system at the Westin? Or did they? Maybe they just have a friend who works at the front desk and was willing to lie... Two, why would they kill Ryan, who was their friend on some level, and who was involved in their criminal enterprise on some level?"

"I suspect it's because up until tonight, he didn't know he was involved with people who resort to murder. Maybe he could turn a blind eye to a little money laundering at Jolly Mon Grill to keep his job. Maybe he was even involved in the money laundering—who knows? But Marcus and Devon realized when he went to negotiate on

Starla's behalf that he knew things they couldn't trust him to stay quiet about."

"That sounds right," I said. "And three, and this is the biggest thing, what is the connection between Jenny and Marcus and Devon?"

"That is indeed the million-dollar question," said Nate. "Speaking of million-dollar questions, they never got back to us. I offered them a million dollars right now. You'd think if nothing else, they'd call back with wiring instructions, take the money."

"They're preoccupied with something," I said.

"You would think we'd be their priority," said Nate. "Perhaps they're understaffed. We need to talk to Jenny."

"I agree with Mamma," I said. "I'm shocked that Jenny was involved with all this. But it does explain several things, like how was Poppy taken so fast."

"That's one mystery solved," said Nate. "I'm wondering if Jenny was somehow coerced, and if she's all right. I wish now I'd dealt with her directly, instead of through the property management company. I don't even have her cell phone number. Not that I suppose she'd answer a call from one of us right now."

I slid Jenny's card—the one I'd taken from her a hundred years ago at breakfast that morning—out of the pocket of my laptop bag and grinned at him. "Why don't we give it a try? She gave me this in case I needed it for a future trip."

"Now that is fortuitous."

She answered on the first ring, her voice tentative. "Hello?"

I put her on speaker. "Jenny? This is Liz."

She burst into tears. "She's in the windmill tower at the Catherineberg ruins."

"We know," I said. "We've already picked her up. Are you all right?"

"Mmm-hmmm." She didn't sound very sure.

"Jenny, *why*?"

"I had no choice." Her voice dissolved into sobs. "They threatened to hurt my grandmother."

What kind of people threatened someone's grandmother? "Where are you now?"

"I'm at home. I live in Coral Bay."

"We'd like to talk to you."

"Where are you?" she asked. "I know you're not at the house. I went back there earlier."

I was wary of her intentions and her loyalties. For all I knew, she'd lead Marcus and Devon straight to us. I looked at Nate.

Nate said, "Jenny, go to Love City Market and wait in the parking lot. We'll send someone to pick you up. She'll give you the password 'candy cane.'"

Nate ended the call.

"Who's picking her up?" I asked.

"One of Bart's team is a woman. I'll ask him to send her. Might be more reassuring than a strange man, though I have no doubt she's every bit as lethal."

"When things settle down, I want to hear more about this team. Maybe actually meet them. But for right now, about Jenny ... if they coerced her once, how do we know they're not doing it again?" I asked. "They could follow her straight to us."

"They might," said Nate. "But we need quick answers, and Jenny's got them. And I have a few tricks up my sleeve. There's no one on our security team who can't spot a tail."

Chapter Nineteen

Earlier, just before Colleen's light show led us to Poppy, I'd started to profile Odella Harrigan. While we waited for Jenny, I turned my attention back to Aunt Odella.

Nate said, "I'm going to talk to the others. We need to get everyone in one spot—even Starla. Bart and I need to figure out some logistics. Should trouble arrive before I get back, fire one shot."

"Will do."

I remembered Mamma saying Aunt Odella's family had been on St. John for ages. And while I did find a Harrigan family, there was no trace of Odella, other than her current driver's license and car registration. Whatever her various entrepreneurial interests were, she made enough money to own—through Phoenix Investments—a gorgeous, six-bedroom villa on Bordeaux Mountain with views that would've pushed the property into the same price range as Nate's house on Cinnamon Ridge.

Whatever her background was, it was well hidden. That, in and of itself, told me a great deal. People who had nothing to hide left more electronic breadcrumbs to follow.

Nate texted me:

> Jenny arriving. I'll meet her in the
> parking lot. Be right there.

I heard a car door close, then another. A few moments later, Nate, Bart, and Jenny walked across the deck.

Nate pulled out a chair for Jenny. "I'm glad to see you're all right."

She collapsed into the chair. "You have to understand. My grandmother is the only family I have left. She raised me. Marcus threatened her."

"Did you believe he would harm your grandmother?" I asked.

"I know he would," she said.

"How do you know Marcus?" I asked.

"We used to date," she said. "Before I knew what he was really like. He's a sociopath. A handsome, charming sociopath."

"Walk me through this, Jenny," said Nate. "How did Marcus, your *former* boyfriend, come to know we were your clients?"

"When we dated, he always asked me questions about

my clients," she said. "Anyone who can hire a private chef has money, right? At first, I thought Marcus was just interested in my day, the way all couples talk about work. But then there were a few too many coincidences ... a couple of my clients were burgled. I think another client was blackmailed after I told Marcus about the girl he was traveling with. She was underage."

Jenny sighed. "We broke up more than two years ago. But Marcus still coerces information from me. He's always threatening me. Anyone I get close to, Marcus uses them against me. He tried paying me for information at first, but I told him I didn't want his money. So now he just threatens me."

"What did you tell him about us?" asked Nate.

"When you first bought the house, he quizzed me about you. I think he keeps a file on people who own property here. He knows if you can afford to buy a house like that—especially if you don't rent it—you have a lot of money. So, he collects information. He would have in his file that you're a private investigator. That's something you told me years ago. There've been tidbits like that. Nothing of any real consequence."

"And more recently?" I asked.

"This morning, Marcus saw the two of you at the Westin talking to the women from Ohio. And he remembered seeing your family at Jolly Mon Grill last night. He came by my house asking all kinds of questions about you, your family, what you've been talking about the last few days."

"And what did you tell him?" Nate asked.

"That y'all met those ladies on the beach, and Mrs. Talbot was helping them spy on one of their husbands," said Jenny.

"How did you know that?" I asked.

"I overheard your mother telling you," she said sheepishly. "I couldn't figure out why Marcus cared about this old man from Ohio and his wife and his mistress. Marcus knew about the pictures Mrs. Talbot took in the restaurant."

I pondered that for a minute. "So, if he were trying to make it look like Melvin Baker had never been here, he knew we have proof to the contrary."

"Oh no," Jenny whispered. "It makes no sense to me why he'd want to do that, but yes, that's right."

Jenny apparently knew some of the story, but not all. Now wasn't the time to fill in the blanks. "Why not just have you lift Mamma's phone?" I asked.

"That was my assignment for the day after Christmas," she said. "Not to take the phone, just delete all those photos and see if she'd sent them to anyone. But then he called this evening and said forget that. He told me to get over to the house and bring Poppy to him, and if I didn't, he would hurt my grandmother. I know he has that in him."

"You gave him my phone number?" I asked.

"I did," said Jenny. "This morning he told me to get him everyone's number in your family. They're in your mother's phone. She left it on a table on the deck while she cleaned the kitchen. It's not password protected."

If he had all our numbers, why had he called me? Maybe it was random.

"Marcus knew Poppy was pregnant because you told him?" Nate asked.

Jenny hung her head. "I told him too much, but not that."

How had Marcus known Poppy was pregnant? Had they chosen her over everyone else in the house because of that? Did that make her a more compelling target?

"Was he supposed to meet you at the sugar mill?" I asked.

"No," said Jenny. "I didn't want to take her. But I knew if I didn't, he'd get someone else to do it. To buy some time, I chloroformed her like he told me—I didn't have time to explain things—and took her somewhere he wouldn't look."

"You just keep chloroform in the medicine cabinet?" asked Bart. "Zip ties in the kitchen drawer?"

"No, of course not," said Jenny. "But he does, and he told me where he'd hidden a key."

"I think there's a problem with that timeline," I said. "You would've had to've gotten here, drugged Poppy, left a note, and gotten her out of here in roughly thirty minutes. And how did you even move her? Poppy is bigger than you are."

"I was five minutes away when Marcus called me, on the way home from dinner with my grandmother," said Jenny. "And Marcus's house is off Highway 206—on the way. As for how I moved her, I grabbed her from behind under her arms and drug her. I'm young and strong, and I was highly motivated. I was very careful with her."

"What about the zip ties?" asked Nate.

"I put the zip ties on after I got her in the windmill tower in case... I honestly don't know why I did that, except it was part of what he told me to do. Look, I was scared out of my mind. And I took a huge risk. I told him that she came to, got loose, and got away from me when I was getting her out of the car. I said she ran off into the woods."

"Getting her out of the car where?" I asked.

"At his mamma's house. I was supposed to leave Poppy with her."

"His mamma?" Nate asked.

I knew before Jenny said the words who that would turn out to be.

"Aunt Odella."

Of course. Aunt Odella surely knew Poppy was pregnant—with Mamma's first grandchild.

Jenny continued. "Devon is his half-brother. Marcus may be a sociopath, but he gets it from his mamma. Or maybe she just trained him well. Whatever he's done, it's because she orchestrated it. He doesn't put his pants on in the morning without checking with her to make sure she's okay with that."

"Did they follow you here?" I asked. "Marcus and Devon?"

"No," she said. "And I left my purse in my car, just in case Marcus somehow put a tracker in it. I left my car keys under the floor mat."

"That was smart," I said. "But you had both those things with you when you dropped Poppy off at Catherineberg, didn't you?"

"I did," she said, "but I had to drive right past there going from your house to his mamma's. I just stopped for a few minutes at the ruins. He would've had to have been watching me every second to've picked up on that, and even then, he'd probably put it down to signal issues."

"So you're reasonably certain they can't track you here?" asked Bart.

"Yes ... reasonably. I am so sorry about all of this," said Jenny. "I came back to the house, to try to find you—tell you what had happened, but you had already left. That's for the best. Listen, I know these people. If Aunt Odella sees you as a threat ... there's no dealing with them. If they say they're going to let you leave if you do this or that, don't believe them. Don't believe a word they tell you. There's a place offshore ... this is a small island. Burial at sea is not uncommon. There's an underwater graveyard. Who knows how many bodies have been buried there over the years? If Aunt Odella needs you to disappear, that's where you'll end up."

"How many people work for Odella?" asked Nate.

"Between all of her businesses, lot of folks. But most of them have no idea about the illegal stuff. She keeps that close. That's just her, Marcus, and Devon."

"Any idea who she's laundering money for?" I asked.

Jenny shook her head. "No, and I don't want to know. And neither do you. All I know is Aunt Odella showed up here ten years ago and started opening businesses. Most people here adore her. Her food's delicious. She gives money to every needy cause. Goes to church on Sunday. And she's sweet as sugar. Unless you cross her. And now I need you to take me back to Love City Market so I can get home before she figures out I have crossed her."

Nate nodded. "That's a good idea." He made a call, then escorted Jenny to the parking lot.

When he came back and sat down, he said, "Bart, could I have five minutes with my wife, please?"

"Of course. I'll go check on the others."

"I have a plan," Nate said when Bart was out of earshot. "Part of it is already underway. But we need Colleen."

"You know she's not like 911," I said. "We can't just call her when we have an emergency."

With a dramatic flourish of silvery light, Colleen appeared. She perched atop the back of the chair Bart had vacated, her feet in the seat. "911, what is your emergency?" She bray-snorted—her signature laugh —exuberantly.

"Seriously?" I asked.

"I was listening ... just waiting for the right moment to make my entrance," she said.

"You know that thought-planting thing you do sometimes?" asked Nate. When Colleen spoke to people who could neither see nor hear her consciously, she planted ideas in their heads they thought were their own. She could also do this with me, which I found unsettling to say the very least.

"*Yes.*..." She drug out the word.

"When we're ready, we need you to give Aunt Odella the idea to look for us here," said Nate. "Make sure she arrives by land and not by sea."

He outlined his plan.

Colleen nodded as he spoke.

I'd not known her to be this cooperative since she revealed herself as a guardian spirit. I knew full well she was up to something.

Chapter Twenty

We gathered on the patio at Mamma and Daddy's cottage. It had the best view of Cinnamon Bay, and though it was nearly midnight, and we couldn't see a solitary thing beyond the sand except the lights of St. Thomas if we looked westward, we stared towards the water. Everyone was there except Nate, Joe, Bart, and the other members of the security team I'd only seen in passing. There were four of them—three male and one female. They all wore pressed khakis and had the look of military training to them.

The scene was something from a movie, possibly one with Matt Damon, or Bruce Willis in it. Everyone knew we were basically bait. But there was no other way out of this. All things considered, everyone was handling the situation pretty well.

Colleen had made herself scarce, to a point. Just so we

knew she was there—and because this was more dramatic than sitting in a hammock—she floated the way she had over the sugar mill, in the shape of a very large, shimmery star.

Blake, Poppy, Mamma and Daddy were in Adirondack chairs at the edge of the patio. Merry, Beverly, Frankie, and I were scattered around a picnic table. Starla perched on the short wall that bordered the outdoor room. After apologizing and attempting to explain she'd been lied to, she was giving Beverly and Frankie a wide berth. For their part, the ladies from the Upstate ignored Starla. They'd been through quite a lot that day.

Nate and Joe had draped army-green wool blankets they'd gotten from the park ranger over their heads to blend better with the greenery, and then crawled into a nearby stand of sea grapes. I wasn't sure where Bart and the rest of the team were, but I knew they weren't very far away.

I was thinking only Nate and I could see Colleen, even in her current form, when Mamma said, "Would you look at that gorgeous star? It's huge. And here on Christmas Eve. Surely that's a sign." She smiled an almost euphoric smile that seemed oddly out of place given the circumstances.

"It's beautiful, Mamma." I glanced at Merry. Had she given Mamma a Valium?

Merry's eyes met mine, and she nodded.

"I wish I'd thought of that," I murmured.

For the next few minutes, we alternated between nervous chatter and anxious silence.

"Oh dear," said Beverly.

"What's wrong?" My alert level could scarcely get any higher.

"*Shoo. Shoo,*" said Frankie.

"We've got company," said Beverly. "This is the first time I've seen goats roaming around."

I returned to my previous level of high alert as four goats sidled up to the far side of the patio. "They're pretty common here."

"Why do there have to be goats, of all things, at this particular moment?" Mamma closed her eyes. She'd had a bad experience with goats a while back, but that was a whole nother story.

One of the goats hopped up on an empty stretch of patio wall near Starla, and the other three followed. Frankie tried again to shoo them away, and then Merry took a turn, but the goats were only encouraged by the attention.

"Y'all, just leave them be," I said. "They're not hurting anything. And if you ignore them, maybe they'll go away."

Starla turned away and gave them the cold shoulder. The closest one licked her on the face. She squealed and swatted at it, but the goat persisted.

"Yeah, ignoring them's gonna work," said Blake.

"Do you have another idea?" I asked.

Blake jerked around to look over his shoulder, then

resettled in his chair, a look of disbelief spread across his face. "What is this? Do they think it's feeding time?"

I scanned the area behind him.

Three donkeys strolled up behind the row of Adirondack chairs and cozied up to Daddy. One of them nuzzled his ear.

Daddy jumped a little and looked over his shoulder. "There's my buddies." Daddy's voice was subdued but held a twinkle of delight. "Hey, fellas."

"What next?" I asked.

"Chickens." Merry pointed with her head. Three large hens clucked as they sashayed across the sand nearby.

"Well, would you look at this?" Aunt Odella strolled casually around the side of the cottage, walked behind the donkeys, and stood front and center—between our group and the beach, with her back to Cinnamon Bay. She swept her arms wide in a gesture that framed the picture before her. Her voice was as sweet as ever. "You all working on a live nativity? You've got your pregnant woman ... a great big star ... I don't know what that's all about ... some donkeys—"

"Rum-pa-pa-pum, witch" muttered Blake under his breath.

There was a rustling noise in the sea grapes. One of the goats nibbled on a leaf. Two others ducked under a limb. One of the guys must've shooed them. The goats shot away from the bush.

Aunt Odella squinted at the sea grapes and leaned

down, then tilted her head sideways. "Gentlemen, I see you in those bushes. Come on out of there."

Nate and Joe crouched as they climbed out of the bushes, then stood. They still had the army blankets draped over their heads.

Aunt Odella cried out in glee. "And there are the shepherds. I just hope there are some wise men here. Don't see any camels. Now, I think we've had a huge misunderstanding, and I just wanted to come on around and see if we can't straighten all of that out. It's almost Christmas Day, for goodness' sake.

"I know you all wanted to get to the airport," said Aunt Odella, "but the ferries have stopped running for the evening. As a goodwill gesture, I've got a boat that can take you all over to the dock at Charlotte Amalie, right near the airport. Then you can be on your way."

Where were Marcus and Devon? Were they on the boat she was talking about?

"We're enjoying our stay at Cinnamon Bay," I said. "It's so relaxing here. And we wouldn't want to be a bother."

"Now, now ... it's no trouble at all. You wouldn't want to decline my offer of hospitality." Her tone was still sweet, but it had an edge.

"We appreciate the offer," said Nate. "But I think we'll pass."

"St. John is a friendly island. But you all have overstayed your welcome," said Aunt Odella. "I'm friendly myself by nature. But I have some business associates who aren't so nice. Trust me when I tell you that you do not want to cross them. Mmm-mmm."

"I'd say you demonstrated your intentions when you kidnapped my wife," said Blake.

"It's a shame it had to come to that," said Aunt Odella. "I really did like you all. You got a real nice family. But you're *nosy*. All of you. Sticking your nose into my affairs was a huge mistake. Everything woulda been fine if you'd just minded your own business. And now your vacation's been interrupted by all this unpleasantness." She raised her voice. "Marcus?"

Marcus came around the other side of the cottage—the goat side. He carried an automatic rifle on a shoulder strap. He made a show of sliding it around in an arc, pointing it at each of us in turn.

"Devon's going to bring a dinghy and take you out to the boat a few at a time," said Aunt Odella. "You all just stay calm, and everything's going to be just fine. We'll get you to the airport safe and sound, and you can fly on out of here." She glanced over her shoulder, as if she expected him to materialize on the beach as she spoke. Then she picked up her phone, tapped a button, and raised it to her ear.

Anger flashed across her face. "Devon! When I call, you answer. Get yourself in here." She ended the call. "He'll be along directly. Everyone, come on down to the beach now."

No one moved.

"I said, 'Everyone, come on down to the beach.' *Now*."

From nowhere, Bart appeared behind Marcus. Lightning fast, he disarmed him.

Marcus twisted around, crouched, and tackled Bart. The two of them thrashed around in the sand. The goats scattered.

"Marcus!" Aunt Odella hollered, panic in her voice. As she watched the fight, she eased to her right, like maybe she was thinking she might have to make a run for it.

None of us made a move to stop her.

"Get him, Marcus!"

She took another step to her right.

Then she backed towards the beach, turned partway around, and looked over her shoulder, scanning the water.

The putter of a small motor reached us, then a dinghy came into view.

"Devon!" Aunt Odella shouted. "Get up here and help your brother."

As the dingy nosed to shore, there were three figures onboard instead of one.

Two men from our security team hopped out, pulled the dinghy onto the sand, and helped Devon—whose hands were zip-tied—ashore.

Aunt Odella's face registered shock, then rage. She darted right, making a run for it.

The donkeys backed into her path.

She zigged to go around, and they outflanked her.

"Move your asses!" she screamed, smacking the one closest to her.

The donkey brayed in protest, but didn't budge.

The chickens went to clucking and bucking and *baawking*. One of them rushed her, and another flapped its wings, flew up, and perched on her head.

"Get off of me!" She screamed and swatted at the chickens.

Uproarious laughter rose from the other side of the patio.

Merry, Beverly, Frankie, and I stood for a better view of the situation. Bart had subdued Marcus, who lay on the ground with his wrists zip-tied behind his back. Three of the goats had him surrounded, while the other stood on his back.

"Get your hands off me!" Aunt Odella screamed, yanking our attention back to her side of the stage, where the two remaining members of the security team apprehended her and secured her hands behind her back.

And that's when a fleet of dinghies landed at Cinnamon Bay. Local police and several government agencies swarmed the beach and took Aunt Odella and her sons into custody.

"Lawyer," Aunt Odella hissed. "You boys keep your mouths shut. Wait for the lawyers. We'll be home by lunchtime." She fixed Nate and me with the most hateful look you've ever seen.

Nate put his arm around my shoulder, and we

watched as they put her aboard one of the dinghies and led Marcus and Devon to separate boats.

"She probably does have good lawyers on retainer," I said. "Not to mention she has friends in very low places."

"Her so-called friends are probably busy finding someone else to wash their money," said Nate. "As I understand it, *our* friends in law enforcement have already raided the salvage yard and Jolly Mon Grill. All her other businesses are next. Whoever she was laundering money for, they'll burn her and move on. Whatever money she had has been seized, and they'll never recoup that loss."

"She planned to get us all on her boat and take us to the graveyard instead of the airport," I said. "What made her think she could pull that off? That her two sons could overpower all of us?"

Colleen popped in beside me. "I can be very convincing."

She bray-snorted, and the donkeys joined in.

Then the goats started bleating, and the chickens clucked.

"*E-liz-abeth Su-zanne Talbot!*"

"Yes, Mamma?"

"Shall we go back to the house now? These goats are causing me to have flashbacks."

"I was just thinking—" Daddy said.

"Stop that right this minute." Mamma raised both her hands. "You are about to exceed the limits of my medication."

Chapter Twenty-One

It was nearly three in the morning before we collapsed into our beds at Cinnamon Ridge. I was exhausted, but too wired to sleep. After dozing a bit off and on, at nine a.m., I gave up and commenced to warming breakfast. Nate was already up and sipping coffee.

"I sent Beverly, Frankie, and Starla home," he said. "They were eager to get back. Beverly needs to see to her kids. Frankie and Starla wanted to spend at least part of Christmas with their families. I guess the last couple of days made us all reflect on what's truly important."

"On our plane? Are you sure it's safe?"

"Oh no." He shook his head. "Two separate chartered flights. Figured it'd be best to give them some space."

I rummaged in the refrigerator.

Jenny had left us a pancetta, leek, and Gruyère quiche, hash brown casserole, fruit salad, and homemade blueberry muffins for Christmas morning breakfast. It did cross my mind that the same woman who'd prepared all of that had chloroformed Poppy, but the food smelled divine, and Jenny had been feeding us ever since we arrived.

After everything was warmed, we gathered around the table and held hands extra tight while Mamma spoke to the Lord, telling him exactly how grateful we were to be together that Christmas morning, with all of us whole and unharmed. Then we piled our plates high and cleaned them. Afterwards, we lingered at the table, rehashing our Christmas Eve in the islands over and over, and stuffing ourselves silly, telling ourselves and each other we'd just have one more bite until every bite was gone.

"Will Jenny be in trouble?" asked Poppy. "I'd hate to think that. She might've saved my life by not taking me to Aunt Odella's house."

Blake said, "You have got to be kidding me. The woman drugged you and dragged you out of here. She tied you up and stuck a rag in your mouth and left you by yourself in that old sugar mill."

"And I'm just fine," said Poppy. "Probably thanks to her. Plus, they threatened her grandmother, Blake."

He shook his head, turned to Nate, then me. "Did y'all tell the police about the kidnapping?"

"Not yet," said Nate. "We'll all have to go in and give statements. It's up to you guys. If you want to leave that part out, it's fine with me. I do believe Jenny was coerced.

That said, I'm sure the authorities will take that into consideration."

"I say we tell them everything," said Blake. "They can decide whether or not to prosecute her."

"I'll tell them what happened," said Poppy. "But I'll also make it clear I don't blame her, and I hope they won't prosecute her."

Blake continued shaking his head.

"I'm going to have to try to make this quiche," said Mamma. "This combination is delicious."

"It's tasty," said Daddy. "Put some more ham in it if you do."

"Daddy, how's your blood pressure lately?" I asked. "Seems like the doctor advised you to watch your sodium. Cured ham is loaded with sodium."

"Tutti, if I didn't have a heart attack last night, I'd say my blood pressure is just fine, wouldn't you?" asked Daddy. "You worry about your own blood pressure, why don't you? Better yet, Nate's. I bet his is sky high."

"Are you suggesting that would be *my* fault?" I asked.

Daddy raised a shoulder, made a little facial shrug. "What's the latest on the Christmas cookies? Here in a little bit, a cookie would go well with another cup of coffee."

"How can you even think about more food?" asked Merry.

"Just planning ahead," said Daddy.

"Nate, I really appreciate you getting Beverly and

Frankie on their way home so quickly," said Mamma. "Goodness only knows what those creatures did with Beverly's poor husband. Do you think they'll ever recover his body? Bless all that poor family's hearts." Mamma shook her head.

"Doubtful," said Nate.

"I just wonder what will happen to that poor little girl," said Daddy.

Mamma drew back and fixed him with a glare that could've frozen Niagara Falls. "You mean the tramp who lured him down here to his death?"

I said, "*Mamma*, you heard what Starla said. Melvin Baker lied to her. She thought he was a widower."

"Hmmpf." Mamma sniffed. "If she dated men born in the same decade as her, she'd be less likely to have this problem."

"Not to sound uncaring," said Merry, "but when do we open Christmas presents?"

Here's the thing about Merry: She's not materialistic at all. She just likes presents. It could be a pretty rock wrapped up in paper with a bow, and she'd love it. Well, there was the sneaky Santa incident a few years back where she ended up with an oil change kit. She wasn't actually thrilled about that. But she just loves presents, giving them and getting them.

"Perhaps we should focus on our own family today," said Mamma. "I'm just so grateful we all made it through last night in one piece. What are y'all thinking? Are we staying until January fourth as we originally planned, or are you ready to go home after our harrowing experience?"

"We'll do whatever y'all like," said Nate. "But I vote we stay and enjoy our vacation. I can make a few changes to our schedule. Those who feel up to it can go sailing. We can spend a day at Virgin Gorda ... there are lots of beaches we haven't seen yet. Other islands to explore ... we have a boat that can comfortably take us to any of the British Virgin Islands. It's larger than the sailboats they use for the day cruises." He looked at Poppy, a question in his voice.

"I'll give it a try," she said.

Because we loved taking day trips to several other islands in the area and scooting around on the water in general, Nate had rented a boat for the two weeks we'd be in St. John. Apparently, he was thinking of buying it. This was a test drive, is what I'm saying, and I could tell he was eager to begin testing.

"I was thinking we'd motor over to Virgin Gorda one morning and moor just off Devil's Bay, near the Baths," said Nate.

Why on earth such a beautiful place was named Devil's Bay was a mystery to me. If I hadn't been suffering exhaustion and PTSD, I might've Googled it. Anyway, I was looking forward to going back there with our family and taking our time meandering through the giant granite monoliths.

"Are we going back to Trunk Bay?" asked Poppy.

"If you'd like," said Nate. "But there's also Maho Bay, Cinnamon Bay, Honeymoon Beach, Hawksnest Beach, and several others. Liz and I like the snorkeling at Water-lemon Cay best—that's near Leinster Bay."

"I was looking forward to doing some shopping," said Mamma. "And I adore reading by this pool. Let's stay. Why give those crooks the satisfaction of ruining our vacation?"

"I say we stay," I said. "Anyone thinking they'd rather not?"

No one spoke up.

"I guess there won't be any more brisket biscuits." Daddy sighed.

"About the presents?" Merry tried again.

"Esmerelda, truly." Mamma's vice dripped exaspera-tion. "Isn't this lovely vacation present enough?"

"Well of course it is, Mamma. But as you can plainly see, there's a pile of presents under that tree, and they're not going to open themselves."

"I thought perhaps most of those were for decora-tion," said Mamma.

We'd drawn names this year, to cut down on the number of things we'd need to pack. But apparently, Santa Claus had left a few other items under the tree.

"I don't think so, Mamma," I said.

"Well then," said Mamma. "I guess we'd better clear the table."

Daddy settled into the family room in front of the Christmas tree. The rest of us pitched in to clean the kitchen. The sliding doors were open wide, as were the windows. This time of year, there wasn't a need for air conditioning in St. John, at least not this high up where we caught an almost continuous breeze. The sky and the sea beyond the deck were a mix of several shades of blue that seemed to belong in an impressionist painting. "O Holy Night" played over the sound system. Peace and joy settled around us all.

"Is that a cat?" asked Daddy.

I turned to look and sucked in a lungful of air, no doubt making a godawful eeeking noise.

A mongoose strolled across the family room.

"*Nate.*"

"No worries." He kept his voice calm, and slowly crept towards the creature. "St. John is full of mongooses. They were brought here to control the snakes back when the island had sugar plantations. I understand they can be domesticated. This one seems pretty tame. Could be someone's pet."

"Could be rabid," said Daddy.

The mongoose scream-hissed at Nate and ran behind the tree, where rustling noises ensued.

Blake, Bart, and Joe moved quickly beside Nate. They all hunched down, arms akimbo, as if ready to tackle the creature.

"What do we do?" asked Blake.

"I'm not sure," said Nate. "This has never come up before."

"Shoo 'im out," said Daddy, as if the solution were obvious.

"Here, kitty, kitty," called Bart.

"It's not a cat," said Nate.

"Do you think he knows that?" asked Bart.

Nate shrugged.

"He's going to tear up the presents," said Merry.

"Here." Mamma pushed in front of the menfolk, a broom in her hand. She stepped to the far side of the tree and made sweeping motions towards the back side. "Get out from back there," she spoke sternly to the mongoose. "Get on. *Get*. Get away from here."

The mongoose shot out from behind the tree and out the sliding door.

"There." Mamma propped the broom against the wall. "I'll just leave this here in case he decides to come back."

"That's the craziest thing," said Nate. "I've never even heard of that happening."

"It's Frank," said Mamma.

"Me?" Daddy scowled. "What did I have to do with it?"

"You're a magnet for random animals. Isn't it obvious?" asked Mamma.

Daddy shrugged as if to allow it was possible she was right.

"I wonder what sort of doctor we should see about a thing like that." Mamma scrutinized Daddy.

"Now can we open presents?" asked Merry.

"There's nothing under there for you but a lump of coal," said Blake. "A big one."

Merry made a face at him.

"How old are the two of you?" asked Mamma.

We settled into places around the tree and worked our way through the pile of presents, opening them one at a time at Merry's insistence, to show what she called "present respect." Santa Claus, who I'm sure was my husband, had gotten everyone Keen hiking sandals. St. John had several beautiful hiking trails, and I knew exploring them was on his agenda.

"Y'all will love seeing the petroglyphs," said Nate.

Daddy looked like he'd bit into a lemon. "What exactly is a petroglyph? I mighta studied that in school, but it's been awhile."

"Pictures carved into rocks, Daddy," said Merry.

"We'll hike down Reef Bay trail," said Nate. "It's a gorgeous walk—not too strenuous. The petroglyphs are near the bottom, at the base of a waterfall."

"Who carved the pictures into the rocks?" Daddy's squint deepened.

"The Taino," said Nate. "They came here from South America in canoes a *loonng* time ago. These carvings are estimated to be from around—depending who you ask— AD 700, maybe earlier."

"What are they pictures of?" asked Daddy.

"The current thinking on that is it's the Taino's dead ancestors," said Blake.

Nate grinned. "You been reading up on it?"

"It's interesting," said Blake. "I'd like to see the carvings."

"Hmmpf." Daddy wore an expression that might've been construed as a lack of enthusiasm.

"Whose turn is it?" asked Merry. "People, we still have more presents to open." She handed Mamma a box and tried mightily to keep our attention from wandering again.

Nate and I had agreed not to exchange gifts that year. The trip was our gift, time with family, the thing we both wanted. And when we'd made that agreement, I was certain we were spending our last dollar on the trip—the last of whatever money Nate had saved over the years.

When the last of the presents were open and the gift wrap gathered up in a trash bag, everyone wandered outside and settled into their chosen spots to stare at the view. Nate and I stretched out on a double lounge chair by the pool. Merry and Joe were on the upper deck, Blake and Poppy under a covered porch on the lower level, Daddy in a hammock, and Mamma nearby in a lounge chair with a book. Bart stationed himself on the corner of the deck closest to the driveway. He was the only one of us who didn't fall asleep—as far as I know. When I woke up three hours later, everyone else was still asleep. Bart was sipping coffee and standing watch.

I quietly slid off the lounger so as not to wake Nate. I stretched and took in the view, astounded all over again at the breathtaking beauty. How blessed I was to be in this magical place with everyone I loved close enough for me to reach out and touch. Almost everyone.

She must have felt me thinking of her.

Colleen walked on water. She literally walked across the pool without leaving a hint of a ripple on the surface.

"Merry Christmas!" she said.

"Merry Christmas."

She sighed, shook her head in an exasperated sort of way. "I'm tired of waiting. Check your pockets. I saw Santa slip something in there."

She slid into the water.

I knew no one else could see her. Colleen couldn't walk on water when she materialized. Nevertheless, I swiveled my head to check. Bart smiled and lifted his chin, way too nonchalant for him to have witnessed Colleen's antics. Everyone else was either out of the line of sight or asleep.

I took two steps to the edge of the pool to see if Colleen might be pulling a mermaid on me, but the water was still and the pool floor void of magical sea creatures.

What was she talking about? Nate and I had agreed on no gifts... I patted my pockets. My hand landed on a flat box. How had I missed this? I pulled it out. It was a robin's-egg blue box with a white satin ribbon. *Tiffany.*

"Oh, my stars," I whispered.

I sat back down on the lounger.

"What'd you find?" Nate stirred, a sleepy grin on his face.

"Sweetheart ... you shouldn't have. We agreed. I don't have a gift for you. I thought... I mean—"

He sat up in the lounger and pulled me close. "Shhh. Enough of that. What I wanted for Christmas was to see your face when you opened one of those blue boxes. Don't disappoint me, now."

I must confess to trembling hands as I pulled the ribbon loose and slid the top off the box. Inside was a circlet choker made of delicate diamonds set in platinum.

I gasped.

He grinned from ear to ear. "Now that's exactly what I wanted, right there."

"Nate... I've never... It's the most beautiful thing. I've never in my life..." I set to babbling.

"Here." His arms came around to envelop me as he lifted the diamonds from the box. "Let me help you with that."

He fastened it around my neck.

A couple happy tears escaped from my eyes.

God bless us every one.

But especially my husband.

Chapter Twenty-Two

On January fourth, after two additional preflight inspections followed by two long test flights, we boarded Nate's plane—our plane—for home. He wanted to be very sure Aunt Odella hadn't somehow had the plane sabotaged after the last time he had it checked, but before she was arrested.

Somewhere over the Atlantic, Nate carried two glasses of Champagne to the back of the plane and sat down beside me. Everyone else was either asleep or using headphones to listen to music or a movie.

"What are we celebrating?" I asked.

"I'm hoping you'll want to toast my proposal," he said.

I'd been waiting for him to bring it back up. "You want to close Talbot & Andrews Investigations."

"Only if that's what you want as well." His eyes held a mixture of hope and love. "Have you thought about it?"

"I have," I said. "I know what we do is dangerous sometimes. And I know it worries our family. We've both had close calls. I'd never get over it if I insisted we continue working as private investigators and then something happened to you. Well... I'd never get over anything happening to you regardless. But, maybe we should stop taking so many risks.

"And I've had a chance to adjust a bit to..." I gestured around the plane. "...all of this. We have the wherewithal to do a lot of good. I think it would be selfish to do anything else, really. We're good at our jobs, but we're not the only PIs in South Carolina. We're possibly in a unique position to benefit Stella Maris."

Nate grinned. "I'd hoped you'd see it that way. So ... we dissolve Talbot & Andrews Investigations, and then we occupy our time studying beach erosion, island evacuation, and all such as that?"

I swallowed. This was hard, but somehow it felt right. "Agreed."

A whirl of silvery, sparkling light swept through the plane.

Colleen appeared in the seat in front of us, standing on her knees. "And *that's* what I've been waiting to hear."

She wore the widest smirk you've ever seen.

This was your end game all along, wasn't it? I threw the thought at her, out of habit more than anything else.

She laughed exuberantly. "Being a detective has been a blast. But now you can work for me full-time."

What on earth had I gotten us into?

"Colleen?" I looked out the window for a moment at the passing clouds.

"What?"

"About that dream..." I'd had a recurring nightmare for years that ended with Nate being washed overboard on a boat as a hurricane closed in on Stella Maris. Colleen may or may not have had something to do with planting that fear.

"That was one scenario," she said. "It's within your power to make sure that never happens, not as a private detective, but as someone who focuses her efforts on evacuation strategies, among other things."

"To the Talbot & Andrews Foundation." Nate lifted his glass and stared into my eyes.

I touched my glass to his, and we drank to our future.

Acknowledgments

My heartfelt thanks to each and every reader who has connected with Liz Talbot and her family. You make it possible for me to spend my days engaged in the happiest endeavor I can imagine—making things up and writing them down. I am truly grateful.

Thank you, Jim, my husband, best friend, and fiercest advocate, for endless encouragement and enthusiasm, and for always serving as my sounding board.

Huge thanks to our dear friends, Don and Gretchen Horan, who helped brainstorm the idea for this book while we were in St. John.

Thank you Beverly Baker and Frankie Summey, who appear as characters in this book because Beverly won a contest and asked Frankie to do this with her. With the exception of a few minor details supplied by Beverly, their story here is wholly a product of my imagination. I so hope you ladies enjoy this story as much as I enjoyed writing it.

Thank you, Tess Thompson, for answering endless questions and holding my hand while I took this leap.

Thank you Gretchen Smith. You know what you did.

Thank you to all the members of The Lowcountry Society, for your ongoing enthusiasm and support.

Thank you Trish Long, for excellent editing in a hurry.

Thank you MaryAnn Schaefer, my able assistant, who seems to work all the time, and must have the lowest hourly wage in the country.

Thank you, Jill Hendrix, owner of Fiction Addiction bookstore, for your ongoing support and encouragement, and for answering endless questions.

As always, I'm terrified I've forgotten someone. If I have, please know it was unintentional and in part due to sleep deprivation. I am deeply grateful to everyone who has helped me along this journey.

About the Author

Susan M. Boyer is the author of the USA TODAY bestselling Liz Talbot Mystery Series which has won or been nominated for honors such as the Agatha Award, the Daphne du Maurier Award, the Macavity Award, multiple Okra picks, and the Pat Conroy Beach Music Mystery Prize. She and her husband call Greenville, SC, home and spend as much time as possible on the Carolina coast.

Look for the first book in a new series from Susan coming in April 2023!

Sign up for Susan's newsletter on any page of her website by scrolling to the bottom or waiting for the pop-up. Susanmboyer.com

The Liz Talbot Mystery Series

Lowcountry Boil (A Liz Talbot Mystery # 1)

Lowcountry Bombshell (A Liz Talbot Mystery # 2)

Lowcountry Boneyard (A Liz Talbot Mystery # 3)

Postcards From Stella Maris (Five Liz Talbot Short Stories)

Lowcountry Bordello (A Liz Talbot Mystery # 4)

Lowcountry Book Club (A Liz Talbot Mystery # 5)

Lowcountry Bonfire (A Liz Talbot Mystery # 6)

Lowcountry Bookshop (A Liz Talbot Mystery # 7)

Lowcountry Boomerang (A Liz Talbot Mystery # 8)

Lowcountry Boondoggle (A Liz Talbot Mystery # 9)

Lowcountry Boughs of Holly (A Liz Talbot Mystery # 10)

Lowcountry Getaway (A Liz Talbot Mystery # 11)

Made in United States
Orlando, FL
04 February 2023

29442078R00125